Praise for

A Trick of the L

2014 ALA Best Fiction for Young Adults

2014 Bank Street College Best Book of the Year

"A painful and necessary account of how eating disorders affect boys, too. Metzger's choice to cast the disease in the role of narrator forces readers inside Mike's head, an extremely uncomfortable yet illuminating way to examine this lethal disease." —*Publishers Weekly* (starred review)

"A unique look at mental illness. This unusual and moving novel addresses complicated ideas, and is ultimately a hopeful tale about coming back to life." — *Philadelphia Inquirer*

"*A Trick of the Light* sheds the spotlight on a little-discussed but surprisingly common condition—anorexia in teen boys. Narrated by the voice inside young Mike's head, the novel inventively presents the private thoughts of a boy whose increasingly distorted image of himself wreaks havoc on his life—and health. A new and important look at an issue that deserves our attention, and compassion."
—Beth Kephart, National Book Award Finalist and author of *Small Damages*

"Metzger's compelling psychological drama takes on the subject of a boy with an eating disorder. The narrative voice—Mike's eating disorder, personified—is the star of this masterfully written novel." —*The Horn Book*

"Many YA books tackle the topic of teens with eating disorders and body image issues. But none combine these elements in quite the same way as Lois Metzger's *A Trick of the Light*. Speaking in a simple, hypnotic style, this unnamed voice distorts logic and warps perceptions, offering Mike the illusion of strength and discipline while pulling him further and further into the depths of anorexia. Don't be misled by the book's small size; this slim volume packs a big emotional punch." —*BookPage*

"*A Trick of the Light* is a marvel. It's hard to imagine a more convincing and insightful depiction of a teenager dealing with a serious personal issue, and yet the story does so in a mysterious and unexpected way. Metzger does a superb job of engaging the reader without revealing any more than is necessary, and the result is a series of surprises that will keep even the most jaded reader going all the way to a realistic and satisfying conclusion."

—Todd Strasser, author of *Fallout*

"A chilling, straightforward novel written with depth and understanding, *A Trick of the Light* shows readers that they must always be vigilant about the voice they listen to—even when it is their own." —*SLJ*

"Metzger's cautionary tale is made more powerful and dramatic by her choice of narrator: the voice in Mike's head. Readers will be easily caught by the quandary: Will the voice prevail, or will Mike recover control of his mind—and his body—before it's too late?" —ALA *Booklist*

"Read in one sitting because I just couldn't put it down. It's short but profound. *A Trick of the Light* will definitely be sticking with me for a long time."

—*Pretty in Fiction*

"The spooky, seductive narrator of Lois Metzger's new book will get inside your head and play tricks on you, just as he does to Mike, the main character. At its heart, though, *A Trick of the Light* is a compassionate and inventive exploration of a little-understood behavior that plagues a surprising number of young men."

—Patricia McCormick, National Book Award Finalist and author of *Never Fall Down*

"The story is well-plotted and its prose engaging. . . . An ambitious and unusual take on teens and eating disorders." —*Kirkus Reviews*

"Mike's warped focus on self-perfection leads him deeper into dangerous and self-punishing anorexia. The use of Mike's commanding inner voice as narrator provides a chilling and distanced narration that effectively conveys the seductive strength of such an impulse. The book manages a rare feat, making Mike's dilemma easy to relate to without making it attractive, and readers will sympathize with Mike and find a new understanding of his problem." —*BCCB*

"A brilliant and powerful piece of writing."

—Richie Partington, "Richie's Picks"

"Mike's world is beginning to spin out of control. But the voice in his head can tell him exactly how to 'master the chaos' in this horror story wrapped in reality. *A Trick of the Light* deserves to stand on the same shelf as Laurie Halse Anderson's *Wintergirls*."

—Richard Peck, Newbery Medal–winning author of *A Year Down Yonder*

"*A Trick of the Light* should be required reading in our schools. Rendered with sensitivity and intelligence, Metzger's beautifully drawn novel illuminates the sneaky-insidious nature of eating disorders with clarity, heart-rending honesty, and hope."

—Robert Crais, #1 *New York Times* bestselling author of *Suspect*

"It provides an accurate and compelling portrayal of an underrepresented population in YA lit, boys with eating disorders; I'm eternally grateful for this. This book was a near perfect read." —*Cornucopia of Reviews*

"The breakout novel *A Trick of the Light* is something both compelling and breathless, yet elegantly written. Lois Metzger may have written a lifesaving book. It never becomes preachy, nor does it provide easy answers, but it looks at the ways teenagers suffer and points a way toward hope."

—Liz Rosenberg, *Barnes and Noble Review*

BOOKS BY LOIS METZGER

NOVELS
Missing Girls
Ellen's Case
Barry's Sister

NONFICTION
The Hidden Girl: A True Story of the Holocaust,
with Lola Rein Kaufman
Yours, Anne: The Life of Anne Frank

EDITOR
Bones: Terrifying Tales to Haunt Your Dreams
Bites: Scary Stories to Sink Your Teeth Into
Be Careful What You Wish For: Ten Stories about Wishes
Can You Keep a Secret?: Ten Stories about Secrets
The Year We Missed My Birthday: Eleven Birthday Stories

A

TRICK

OF

THE

LIGHT

LOIS METZGER

Balzer + Bray

An Imprint of HarperCollins*Publishers*

A Trick of the Light

Copyright © 2013 by Lois Metzger

www.epicreads.com

Library of Congress Cataloging-in-Publication Data
Metzger, Lois.
  A trick of the light / Lois Metzger. — 1st ed.
      p.   cm.
  Summary: Fifteen-year-old Mike desperately attempts to take control
as his parents separate and his life falls apart.
  ISBN 978-0-06-213309-0
  [1. Family problems—Fiction.   2. Anorexia nervosa—Fiction.
3. Eating disorders—Fiction.   4. High schools—Fiction.   5. Schools—
Fiction.]   I. Title.
PZ7.M5677Tri 2013
[Fic]—dc23   2012019039
                                                          CIP
                                                           AC

Typography by Ray Shappell

14 15 16 17 18 CG/RRDH 10 9 8 7 6 5 4 3 2 1

First paperback edition, 2014

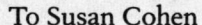

To Susan Cohen

CONTENTS

PART 1

THE MIRROR

CHAPTER 1

THE FIRST TIME I REACH MIKE WELLES, HE'S IN A tunnel. It's hot, syrupy hot, July hot, the kind of heat where your breath going out feels the same as the air going in, or so I imagine. I've been trying to talk to Mike but he can't hear me or can't listen—the distinction isn't important. How long has it been—weeks or months, days? Time is a syrupy thing, too, not always so easy to pin down.

Mike is walking with his best friend, Tamio Weissberg, in the long tunnel beneath the expressway. There's pigeon crap pretty much everywhere, which has earned this place a nickname: the stinky tunnel. They just saw *King Kong*, the original 1933 version, at You Must Remember This, a neighborhood place that shows only the classics. This is far from the first time Mike and Tamio have seen *King Kong*, which they hail as the masterpiece of something called stop-motion animation. But it's their first time seeing it in a movie theater and, needless to say, they were the only ones in the audience without gray hair.

They have to talk loudly because of the whooshing cars overhead, and their voices echo against the concrete walls.

Tamio: "That's the best death scene in movies. Nobody dies like Kong."

Mike: "Every time I keep hoping that he won't die. It's so stupid."

I couldn't agree more. It's a movie. It will never change. But other things can change. I wish I could tell Mike that.

Mike: "The expression in his face is so amazing—how'd they do that? He's just a little model of a gorilla, but he looks really, truly in love. Love at first sight, poor guy."

Tamio: "On the big screen you really notice his fur moving around. You can practically see fingerprints on him."

Mike: "Well. You can't help that. When you handle the model—"

Tamio (shaking his head): "Hair spray. Then the fur won't move as much."

Mike is always impressed by Tamio's knowledge of what seems like everything. This summer they're working at a baseball camp for all of July and half of August, along with a kid named Ralph Gaffney. They're counselors for the six- and seven-year-olds. It also impresses Mike how much the little kids love Tamio, how they beg to help him with the equipment. They're actually disappointed when they can't carry buckets of balls. And when they skin their knees, like a little kid named Ezra did this afternoon, they don't want to cry in front of Tamio.

Mike: "You know, when Ezra got hurt, Ralph couldn't care

less—he just got mad because it was taking too long to wash the blood off and put on a Band-Aid."

Tamio: "Ralph's an asshole. Poor Ezra. Did you tell him he shouldn't have been trying to steal third?"

Mike: "Not only that, but he was sliding."

Apparently they're not supposed to slide until they know how to do it right.

Tamio: "Ezra's a nice kid, but he thinks he's in the majors. When I pitch to him, he tries to tell me how to throw a slider. Hey, watch out!" He pushes Mike away from a ton of pigeon crap.

Mike: "Thanks, you saved my life." He laughs. But he doesn't feel like it. I can tell. I know everything there is to know about Mike Welles.

Why Mike doesn't feel like laughing:

Sometime in June, Mike's mom, Regina Welles, known as Gina, a professional organizer, started sleeping whenever she wasn't helping people clean out their closets, and at night began taking baths that last so long, the water must be cold by the time she finally climbs out. Around the same time, Mike's dad, Douglas Welles, lawyer, started going to the gym. He spends so much time there that Mike hardly sees him.

I don't know why this bothers Mike. He should relish the freedom all of it gives him. But he can't resist his natural urge to talk to Tamio.

Mike: "Things have been kind of weird at home."

Tamio: "Yeah? How so?"

Don't.

Mike stops walking.

Tamio: "What's the matter?"

Mike stares ahead blankly.

Tamio: "Are you all right?"

Mike is thinking about how he just heard a voice in his head. A whisper of a voice, but definitely a voice.

Tamio: "What do you mean, things are weird at home?"

Don't talk about it.

Mike still can't move, stuck in the stinky tunnel. He thinks, Am I crazy?

Tamio: "Hey, what's going on?"

Mike: [nothing]

Tamio: "Dude. Say something."

Mike: "It's nothing."

Mike knows something's wrong but doesn't know where to turn. He thinks things are bad and can only get worse. He has no idea what achievements are within his reach, what rewards await him, how much better his life is going to be.

Infinitely better.

CHAPTER 2

MIKE LIVES WAY OUT IN BELLE HEIGHTS, IN A FAR
corner of Queens that he dislikes and finds dull and frustrating.
You take buses everywhere in Belle Heights; you spend a lot of
time waiting for buses. Mike thinks there's nothing to do here
except wait for the bus. It's a long subway ride away from Manhattan,
and nobody from Manhattan goes to Belle Heights unless they're
driving through it to get to the airport.

But Mike should be perfectly happy with Belle Heights. So what
if nothing happens? You make your own excitement; you create
your own drama. You can live the life you are supposed to live
without the distraction of a bustling city or the so-called charm of
a country village or the smugness of the suburbs. Belle Heights has
a pleasantly anonymous quality. Planes are constantly overhead,
which creates a whooshing sound in the sky; the Belle Heights
Expressway is always crowded, creating a whooshing sound on
the ground. Some streets are as hilly as roller coasters because back

in the Ice Age glaciers traveled south, pushing rocks and sand and clay in front of them, and the glaciers stopped here before moving up north again. They left all their glacier junk behind, right here in Belle Heights. Mike learned this in earth science last year and found it boring, of course. There's so much beauty here—sights, smells, sounds—but he's blind and deaf to it. He needs to open his eyes, get some poetry in his soul. It's something for him to look forward to.

Mike was born in Belle Heights Hospital on March 9, fifteen years and four months ago, on an unseasonably warm day for spring, or so his mom tells him. He's spent his whole life on Belle Heights Road, a curving street with two-story brick houses, each attached on one side to another two-story brick house, and each with a small patch of semi-neglected lawn. Despite the nearness of the neighbors, Mike only knows them to wave and say hi, if anything at all. Once a family moved in halfway down the block and Mike thought the people moving out were the new people coming in.

I think parents generally do their children more harm than good, and Mike's parents are no exception. They don't seem to care about him. They all go to a movie, and Mike's dad says it's hilarious while Mike's mom finds it upsetting. They argue. Does either of them even ask Mike what he thinks?

Mike grew up with one grandparent, Grandma Celia, who died a year ago—or was it two years? Grandma Celia lived in one of those assisted-living facilities, but Mike's dad always said:

"We do all the assisting! She calls here for everything, and when she does, it's like a fire alarm! If she drops something behind a bureau and can't reach it, we go and get it for her. If she needs something at the pharmacy, she hurt her ankle, so we go to the pharmacy for her."

Mom: "She's eighty-six." (Or seven, or eight.) "If she's hurt—"

Dad: "The pharmacy's right in the building—next to the beauty parlor. She gets her hair done every day, doesn't she? The ankle doesn't stop her then. What about the time she thought her brooch was stolen and she wanted you to question the neighbors?"

Mom: "Well. I didn't have to do that."

Dad: "Only because you found it before you had to go door-to-door and interrogate the other little old ladies. What'd she want you to do, slam them up against a wall, shine a light in their eyes?"

Mom: "She's my mother. How can I say no to her?"

Dad: "By saying no, that's how." Good point. "She makes you crazy. I'm just trying to spare you the insanity."

Mom: "I'd like to say no to her. But . . . I can't."

Mike was always surprised by how helpless his mom was when it came to her own mother. She's a professional organizer, but she was totally out of her depth here.

Another time Grandma Celia swore she saw a mouse in her room. Mike's mom has a phobia about mice, which is why they got a cat, Mighty Joe Young (Mike named him after a kind-hearted gorilla in another old stop-motion movie). Mike went with his mom up to Grandma Celia's and looked everywhere for the mouse. When they couldn't find it, Grandma Celia didn't seem all that surprised; she just shrugged and said, "Maybe there was no mouse. . . . It must have been a trick of the light."

Mike knew, then, there had never been a mouse.

If I had to pick, I'd say Mike's dad is the better of the two. Not that he deserves a World's Best Dad coffee mug, but he doesn't talk Mike's ear off and he gives Mike a lot of room. Mike's mom is a different story.

When Mike was in second grade, his teacher—Ms. Jackson? Ms. Johnson? Mike's memories are sometimes spotty—called his mom and said Mike didn't have any friends because nobody understood what he was saying. Mike sat by himself, she said, popping CDs into a CD player so he didn't have to talk to anyone: "He's our little disc jockey." Mike's mom went into overdrive, researching like crazy, interviewing doctors. She got Mike's hearing tested and it was fine—Mike raised his finger to show that he heard all the little beeps and tones he was supposed to hear. She took Mike to several speech therapists before getting a diagnosis of lazy lip syndrome, which meant he wasn't putting enough air into his speech, or some such nonsense. Doctors aren't to be taken seriously. A lazy lip? It's the dumbest thing I ever heard.

Three whole years of speech therapy followed, closely supervised by his mom—enunciation exercises, word repetitions (bus, ball, boy, pants, party, private), looking in the mirror and watching his mouth while reciting something everybody knows, like the Pledge of Allegiance. Even now, though Mike is supposedly cured, he can be hard to understand when he gets tired or scared, and people often ask him to repeat himself or speak up. Even his parents don't always understand him. Except for Tamio, Mike thinks, who always understands him. But I'm not sure Tamio ever really understood Mike. Not deep down, where it counts. The way I do.

Tamio says he and Mike are like unrelated twins. But they're not. Not psychologically, emotionally, or even physically. Tamio is half Japanese, half Jewish, with thick, black hair that goes halfway down his back. Mike has hair and eyes the color of a paper bag. Mike is the taller of the two, but Tamio's in good shape—that's the biggest physical difference between them. Lately Mike's been eating a lot, mostly junk food, and sitting around the house. His belly is starting to stick out over his shorts and he gets winded easily. It's disheartening that Mike has gotten to this point. That he's become so lifeless. Even with his height, Mike feels almost invisible next to Tamio.

Mike met Tamio on his first morning of sixth grade in Belle Heights Middle School. Mike sat at his desk, drawing a Cyclops with two heads.

Tamio: "What is that?"

Mike: "It's a Cyclops with two heads." He waited for Tamio to find him weird and walk away.

But Tamio stayed where he was. "That's an improvement over the usual variety. This one would have depth perception. Pretty badass." He nodded. "Did you ever see *The Seventh Voyage of Sinbad*?"

Mike: "I love that movie!"

What followed was an endless discussion of stop-motion

animation and its god, Ray Harryhausen, who learned the craft from Willis O'Brien, the creator of King Kong.

What is stop-motion? I've heard it more times than I want to remember. That is a problem with memory: sometimes you forget what you wish you hadn't; other times you can't forget something you'd prefer to be rid of.

Stop-motion is using cinematic techniques to create the illusion of movement in an inanimate object. First you make a small model of a giant creature, such as, in the case of King Kong, an eighteen-inch-tall gorilla. You film a frame, walk to the gorilla, move the gorilla a fraction, walk back to the camera, film the next frame, then walk back to the gorilla, move the gorilla again, walk back to the camera, film the next frame, and repeat this over and over and over. Because there are twenty-four frames for one second of film, you have to move the gorilla twenty-four times for only one second of stop-motion animation. All that incessant handling is why the fur—without hair spray, apparently—moves around so much.

I wonder if on some level Mike feels eternally grateful to Ray Harryhausen for bringing him a friend. I suspect, also, that Mike feels grateful to Tamio, who apparently gave up the chance to be everybody's best friend by sticking with Mike.

Tamio is content with Mike the way he is. He once told Mike, "There's a lot of assholes out there—kids who are mean, kids who lie, kids who brag all the time. You're the least assholey kid I know."

What a waste, for Mike to settle for that.

CHAPTER 3

BY THE TIME MIKE GETS HOME, HE'S PRETTY NEARLY convinced himself he didn't hear me at all. This doesn't surprise or discourage me—two steps forward, one step back.

He finds his mom in a panic.

Mom (shouting): "I can't find my book!"

She keeps all her work in a big binder, which she calls her book. It's got clients' names, appointments, billing information.

Mike: "Where'd you see it last?"

Mom: "If I could remember that, do you think I'd be in this situation?"

Mike: "Just asking. That thing's as big as a phone book."

Mom: "Well, it's still missing! I've been scouring the place for an hour. Where is it?"

Mike leans down to pet Mighty Joe Young, who runs away. He's black with a little dribble of white on his chin. It makes him look like he never washes his face, even though that's practically all he does.

Mom: "I can't believe this. If I don't find that book . . . I've got a client in an hour . . . at least I think I do."

Mike knows this isn't like her. She always has her day's schedule memorized and is never late.

Mike: "I'll help you find it, okay?"

She doesn't even say thanks.

Mike's house has two bedrooms upstairs, plus a small room his dad uses as a home office. It's the first place Mike decides to look. The door is closed and he knocks.

Dad (from inside): "Yeah?"

Mike: "Can I come in?"

Dad (pause): "Sure."

Mike opens the door and almost doesn't recognize his own father. What's different? Mike is reminded of those trick photographs that appear in magazines side by side—at first they seem identical, but if you look closely you can spot ten differences.

It's the glasses, Mike realizes. His dad used to wear plain wire rims; these are thick, black plastic, with an anti-reflective coating so you can see his brown eyes.

Mike: "You got new glasses."

Dad: "Yes." He leans his hands on his desk. There are piles of papers everywhere: on the shelves, on top of the printer. Mike's mom calls this "vertical mess." Mike's dad has a collection of heavy brass paperweights. A hunting dog in the pointer position is balanced on top of a particularly huge pile.

Mike doesn't like his dad's new glasses. He's not sure why.

Mike: "Why'd you change your glasses?"

Dad (hesitates): "I needed a new prescription."

Mike: "You didn't have to change the frames."

Dad (tightens his lips): "What do you want, Mike?"

Mike: "I'm looking for Mom's book."

Dad: "Why?"

Mike can't believe it. His mom's been searching for an hour and his dad has no idea.

Mike: "Because it's missing."

Dad: "Why would her book be in here?"

Mike: "Because it isn't anywhere else."

Dad: "Well, it's not here."

Mike: "Are you sure?"

Dad: "Yes. Look, let me finish up. I've got to get to the gym before six."

There's an ache inside Mike. He doesn't know why.

Go with him.

Though Mike on principle doesn't like the idea of listening to a voice in his head, he thinks it might be on to something here.

Mike: "Can I go with you?"

Dad: "What?"

Mike's not sure if his dad didn't understand him or if he's just questioning why Mike wants to go. To be safe, Mike remembers his lazy-lip exercises and speaks slowly and carefully: "Can I go to the gym with you?"

Dad: "Why? You never wanted to before."

Mike doesn't know what to say. He says, "I have to work out."

Dad: "Why, do you think you're fat?"

Mike grabs his belly, surprised there's so much to grab. At least Mike is realizing how far he's been letting himself go.

Mike: "Yeah."

Dad: "You're not fat."

Mike: "Please take me with you."

Dad: "You're not a member."

Mike: "Can't I go as a guest or something?"

Dad: "I don't know if the gym allows guests."

Mike: "Can't you at least call and ask?"

Dad: "I don't know if the gym allows children."

Mike: "Children! I'm fifteen!"

Dad: "Forget it, Mike."

What's with him? Mike wonders. It's like there's a wall around him and you can barely see over the top. Mike can't shake the feeling that a few months ago his dad would've said, "Sure, c'mon, let's go."

When Mike gets back to the living room, his mom is holding the book to her chest.

Mike: "Where was it?"

Mom: "Hidden in plain sight! Actually, you gave me the idea. You said it was as big as a phone book, and there it was, in the pile of phone books. I guess I had to look up a number and stuck it in there without thinking." She sighs. "Thanks for trying to find it."

Mike: "I only looked in Dad's room. He got new glasses."

Mom: "I know."

She doesn't sound too fond of them, either.

CHAPTER

4

MIKE IS STANDING JUST OUTSIDE A FLEA MARKET. There's one every week in a fenced-off vacant lot on Belle Drive. His mom says that flea markets are like crack for people with a clutter problem. They feel compelled to go in and buy something they don't need and have no room for that will only make their lives worse.

It's late August. Camp is over and Tamio's in Japan, where he goes at the end of every summer. Mike finally received his schedule for tenth grade. He's got three classes with Ralph Gaffney and none with Tamio, not even lunch. He and Tamio play on the high school baseball team (Tamio, third base; Mike, right field) but workouts don't start until December. Mike feels adrift with nothing holding him steady.

Girl's voice: "Are you staring at me?"

Mike blinks a couple of times. He didn't see her before, but there's a girl in front of him.

Girl: "Why are you staring at me, Mike?"

He knows her. It's Amber Alley. He and Amber have gone to the same schools since kindergarten.

Mike: "I'm not staring at you."

Amber: "I can always tell when someone's staring at me. I can feel it."

Mike finds Amber strange. He sees her stringy black hair that hangs down in her eyes, and notices she's wearing a big long-sleeved shirt and baggy pants even now, when it's a hundred degrees. She looks lost in her own clothes, he thinks.

But she's not. She's beautiful.

Amber: "What are you doing here, then?"

Mike: "I'm buying cat food."

Amber: "At a flea market?"

Mike: "I just stopped for a second. Because it's so hot."

Amber breathes out and the air in front of Mike smells like cinnamon. "Do you have a cat?"

Mike: "Yeah, I have a cat."

Amber (pointing to a thick brown thing around her neck): "Look, I just got this cool necklace. From that lady over there, the one who looks like a Gypsy, see?"

But Mike isn't looking for the Gypsy; he's looking at Amber's eyes, at how flat and shiny they are, like glass. At first he wonders if she's wearing contacts, but Tamio wears contacts and his eyes don't look like that. Mike doesn't see it, but actually her eyes look exotic, otherworldly.

Amber: "This is pure copper. Do you know what a healing object is?"

Mike (bored): "Something to heal you when you're sick?"

Amber: "That's medicine. A healing object is something that helps you become the person you are meant to be." Mike doesn't know what she's talking about. "Do you remember the butterflies?"

Mike: "What?"

Amber: "The butterflies! From third grade, Ms. Taylor's class? You were my butterfly partner."

Mike (dimly): "Right."

They were butterfly partners! That's perfect.

Amber: "Everybody in the class got paired off and was given a caterpillar. We had to take notes on it, what it ate and everything. We named ours Rainbow Sue."

Mike remembers that he wanted to name it Mothra, but Amber insisted.

Amber: "She was in a cocoon for three weeks. She was the last one in our class to pop out, and when she did, she was so beautiful, orange and black. Then Ms. Taylor took us all outside and we released the butterflies—then pigeons swooped down and ate them! It was horrible!"

Mike remembers. Amber cried so much, her mom had to come pick her up.

Amber: "Rainbow Sue was born and died on the same day. She was supposed to fly to Mexico. Why'd we go to all that trouble? We raised her up just to get eaten by pigeons. Do you think our lives are like Rainbow Sue's?"

Mike: "I don't think so. I mean, I don't know. I can't discuss the meaning of existence in hundred-degree heat."

Amber's always by herself at school, and Mike thinks he's beginning to understand why. But her solitude doesn't surprise me. It's always the most interesting people who have a hard time fitting in, but they go on to lead the most extraordinary lives.

Amber: "So, how's your summer been?"

Mike thinks about how his crappy summer has only gotten worse. His mom cancels nearly all her appointments now, and is either asleep or in the tub, so Mike has to do the laundry and grocery shopping or they'd have nothing clean to wear and nothing to eat. And his dad's never home, and Tamio's halfway around the world, and when school starts he'll never get to see Tamio—

Talk to her.

Mike tenses up.

You can trust her.

I'm louder and clearer right now than I've ever been. It's so satisfying! But there's a catch of panic in Mike's throat. He is hoping desperately that the voice he hears is just a bizarre product of the heat. And he wonders why it would tell him not to talk to Tamio, and now it's telling him to confide in the weirdest girl he knows.

Amber: "Mike?"

Mike: "My summer's been good. You?"

Amber: "Oh, fantastic!"

Mike should be curious about her fantastic summer, but he's not.

Mike: "Maybe I'll go in and look around."

Amber: "You want a healing object?"

Mike: "Maybe."

Amber: "Okay. See you at school. You taking physics this year?"

Mike: "Yeah, in the afternoon."

Amber: "Me, too."

Mike's thinking, Oh, no, classes with Ralph and Amber. He doesn't yet see why she's so special. She's not typical Belle Heights. She doesn't seem to belong to any specific time or place. He should feel such a connection to her—if you believed in past lives, you'd think she and Mike were once related.

But Mike has already forgotten her now that he's in the flea market. There's a whole table of tube socks, six for a dollar. A big chair with stuffing bursting out. Stacks of old rock albums. The Mamas & the Papas are looking up at Mike. Mike wonders why there's a fat kid standing right next to him, looking at The Mamas & the Papas, too. . . .

He can't believe it.

He's looking in a mirror.

The fat kid is himself.

The mirror is leaning against a table. It's tall and narrow, about three feet by one foot. The wooden border looks rotted and splintery, but that's not important. Mike looks at himself again. How did this happen? He was weighed last spring at the doctor's office and was average then; how did he go from average to fat so quickly? He thinks about what he had for lunch: two burgers and double fries.

You need to buy this mirror. So you can keep an eye on yourself.

He's a little less frightened by me. He's beginning to wonder if

I'm right, if maybe I have his best interests at heart. He's not sure. But he is sure that he wants the mirror.

Mike (to a woman in a lawn chair, next to the mirror): "How much?"

Woman (frowning): "You want to buy the mirror?"

Mike notices a table full of sunglasses. So the mirror's just there for people to see how they look in sunglasses. It doesn't matter.

Mike: "Yeah, I want to buy the mirror."

Woman: "Isn't there a price tag on it?"

She's stalling. She knows there isn't a price tag and she can see how much Mike wants it. Mike looks for a price tag and finds only a rusty wire in the back.

Mike: "There's no tag."

Woman: "It must've fallen off. Well, it's eleven dollars."

That's a lot, he thinks; he can buy sixty-six tube socks for that much. He looks in his wallet. There's two fives and a single—it's a sign! There are also some singles shoved in his pocket. Still. He has the exact amount in his wallet, where money is supposed to be.

Mike: "I'll take it."

She wraps up the mirror in some old newspaper. Mike notices the date—sometime in May, before his mom started hibernating and soaking, and his dad started going to the gym. Mike tucks the mirror under his arm and heads out. On the way home, he passes a woman with a pigeon on her shoulder. At least he thinks it's a pigeon, until it talks and he realizes it's a parrot.

Bird: "What's the matter? What's the matter?"

Mike thinks about the fact that this woman has a voice on her shoulder, but she can go home and put it in a cage. He wonders if there's a cage that can hold the voice in his head.

He doesn't understand. Not yet.

CHAPTER 5

MIKE POUNDS A NAIL INTO HIS BEDROOM WALL, and the sound drives Mighty Joe Young under the bed. Most of Mike's walls are covered by Mets posters, but there's a tall, empty rectangular space just opposite his bed. The mirror fits the space perfectly, as if it was waiting for it.

Mom (standing in doorway): "You woke me."

Mike: "Maybe you shouldn't be sleeping in the middle of the day."

Mom (either not hearing or ignoring Mike's comment): "What are you doing?"

Mike: "I got a mirror."

Mom: "I can see that. But why? Oh, you're bleeding."

Mike looks down and is surprised to see blood all over his finger.

Mom: "Don't wipe it on your pants! No wonder you cut yourself—the wood's coming off in splinters." She pokes around the mirror. "The wire's all rusty. When's the last time you had a tetanus shot?"

Mike (remembering): "In the spring."

Mom: "Why did you get this, if it's warped?"

Mike: "Warped?"

Mom: "Definitely. The glass is wavy. Look how wide you look."

Mike (sadly): "That's what I look like."

Mom: "No, it isn't. Where'd you get it?"

Mike knows she wouldn't like the truth. He could lie. It would be so easy. But Mike hasn't ever been a good liar.

Mike: "A flea market."

Mom (as if pierced to the heart): "No! How much did you pay?"

Mike: "Eleven dollars."

Mom: "You got robbed." She sighs. "Could you call my four o'clock for me? I'm not going to make it."

Mike sighs too.

Mom: "Did you pick up the Feline Fine?"

Mike remembers the cat food he was supposed to buy.

Mike: "Ahh, no. I totally forgot."

Mom: "You'll have to go out again."

Mike: "I know."

Mom: "Where'd you put the laundry? I looked on the shelf—"

Mike: "It's on top of the machine, already folded. I didn't put it away yet."

Mom: "Oh, and Mighty Joe Young threw up near the couch."

The cat throws up a lot. It's disgusting, the way Mighty Joe Young walks backward while he's doing it. Tamio once said, "He looks like a movie of a cat eating, on rewind." Mike laughed, but there's nothing amusing about the fact that he has to clean up cat vomit all the time.

Mike: "Mom, I already cleaned up after him twice today."

Mom: "But . . . could you, again? I can't."

Mike: "Fine."

Look at yourself—running errands, doing laundry, cleaning up cat vomit. Is this the person you are meant to be?

Mike thinks the voice in his head must hate him. But I don't. I'm the best thing that ever happened to him.

CHAPTER 6

JUST AS IT'S ALL COMING TOGETHER, LIKE A PAINTING that looks like random dots until you step back and see the whole glorious scene, the worst possible thing happens.

Mike falls in love.

It's not love, of course—it's idiotic teenage infatuation and will lead only to rejection and heartbreak—but Mike is convinced it's the real thing and he won't listen to reason.

It's the first day of tenth grade, homeroom. Mr. Clayton, his homeroom and physics teacher, is standing at the front of the room with a girl taller than he is.

Mr. Clayton: "This is Valerie Braylock."

Mike instantly adores everything about Valerie Braylock, including the fact that she's a giant. She's African American with dark-gray eyes much too big for her face, but Mike thinks they're beautiful, the color of smoke. Dark, curly hair spills over her shoulders and Mike is gone, absolutely gone.

Mr. Clayton: "She's new."

Valerie: "Well. I'm new to Belle Heights, and new to Belle Heights High School, but I'm not new to myself."

What is that supposed to mean?

Even some of the girls exchange looks. Melissa Sacks, who is the first-ever sophomore to be named yearbook editor, rolls her eyes at the Rubys. Ruby Lobenhoffer and Ruby Cutler, known as Ruby L and Ruby C, are inseparable best friends and Melissa Sacks devotees. Mike notices this and thinks they're jealous of Valerie's stunning beauty.

Mr. Clayton: "Valerie just moved here from Spruce Hills."

Spruce Hills is a Q22 bus ride away from Belle Heights, a neighborhood with a new shopping mall that includes a Target and a Home Depot. When Mike and Tamio went to see it, Tamio said, "Welcome to the world of tomorrow!" I don't know why Mike finds Tamio funny; his jokes don't make any sense. Anyway, Mike never thought much of Spruce Hills until this moment, when Spruce Hills became the birthplace of Valerie Braylock.

Mr. Clayton: "I hope you'll all try to make her feel welcome."

Mike is more than ready to take on the job of welcoming committee. Do I need to mention that Mike has never had a girlfriend? As soon as homeroom is over, he rushes to her like the proverbial moth to the flame. She towers over him, and Mike is immediately caught in her sweet, flowery fragrance.

Mike (drunkenly): "Hi, my name is Mike Welles and I just want to say, you know, hi."

Valerie: "What?"

Mike (slowly and carefully): "My name is Mike Welles. Hi."

Valerie: "Hi."

Mike: "What's your schedule? Maybe we have some classes together. That way if you have any questions I can, you know, help you out."

They compare schedules. Or, rather, Valerie looks at Mike's schedule while Mike looks at Valerie. Close up he notices her smooth skin, and a tiny scar below her left cheek.

Valerie: "We have physics, last period."

Mike: "That's great! If you, you know, need help after school, I could, you know . . ."

Valerie: "Actually I'm a dancer, and I have to go to class after school every day."

Mike (as if she couldn't get any more wonderful): "You're a dancer?"

Valerie (nodding): "Ballet."

Mike: "Wow. Just . . . wow."

She's way too curvy to be a ballet dancer. The bell rings.

Mike: "Anyway, see you in physics."

She smiles briefly and leaves. Mike thinks her smile is like the sun and the stars and the entire Milky Way. I try to warn Mike of the pain that awaits him with this girl, but he's lost in daydreams. His visions of him and her together are too absurd to describe.

He texts Tamio about being in love with Valerie Braylock.

Tamio texts back that she's in his math, English, and music appreciation classes, and also his lunch period. Mike is instantly jealous.

Tamio (text): She's cute.

Mike: I saw her 1st.

Tamio: She's all yours.

Mike: U better believe it.

I don't like anything about this. Girls flock to Tamio. What will happen to Mike when Valerie invariably does the same?

The day is uneventful, just the usual high school nonsense. Ralph Gaffney is wearing a T-shirt that says I'M NOT AS THINK AS YOU DRUNK I AM, and Melissa Sacks reports him, explaining to the Rubys, "I texted my mom. As head of the PTA she says that even though we don't have a dress code per se, we can't allow clothing that promotes substance abuse. If Ralph doesn't change his shirt, my mom will take it up with the school board." Melissa can't stand Ralph because last year she and the Rubys made a video of themselves dancing (it was called "The Belles of Belle Heights") and posted it on YouTube. Ralph wrote something so pornographic in the comments section that Melissa had the video removed. Well, she's having her revenge now. Ralph has to borrow a shirt from the lost & found, which already has clothing in it on the first day of school.

By the time physics rolls around and Mike sees Valerie again, her hair is in a tight bun. Mike can barely catch his breath. Now he has a different image to add to his collection.

Mike (rushing up to her): "How's your first day been?"

Valerie: "Fine! Everyone's been really friendly."

Mike is sure all the boys have been friendly, at least.

Mike: "Your hair's different."

Valerie: "I have to wear it like this for dance."

Mike notices that beneath her button-down shirt, there's a scoop neckline that wasn't there before.

Mike: "You have a change of clothes on, under?" He instantly regrets saying that.

Valerie (not upset): "I have my leotard and tights on. That way, when I get to the studio, I can rip my clothes off and be ready for class."

Mike is practically hyperventilating.

Valerie: "I can't be late—in fact I have this recurring nightmare of being late. There's a performance and I'm not in costume because my hair's not ready or something, and the music's starting. The whole ballet is ruined because of me."

Mike wishes he had a recurring nightmare he could tell her about.

Speaking of late, Amber walks into the physics lab right now. She scoots into a seat at a table diagonally in front of Mike. He can smell her cinnamon smell. Melissa Sacks, up front where she always sits, turns around to look at the Rubys and pretends to stick her finger down her throat. Amber makes Melissa want to throw up, apparently. These girls are so shallow. Amber is so much deeper than any of them could ever hope to be.

Mike goes to Tamio's house after school. Tamio lives four blocks from Belle Heights High, on Seventy-Fifth Crescent, which means crossing Seventy-Fifth Road, Seventy-Fifth Circle, and Seventy-Fifth Street. It's another two long blocks before you get to anything with a seventy-six. All the streets in Belle Heights are that way. Places are never exactly where you think they'll be.

It's Tamio's mother's birthday and there's a party in their sunny dining room, where the walls are covered with framed pictures of flowers. There's pizza, cake. Mike devours several slices of pizza. He sees Tamio's parents, how different they look (he's tall with curly brown hair; she's tiny with short black hair), how easy they are with each other, always a hand on the arm, a whisper, a laugh. Mike wonders about the last time he heard his parents laugh. He feels a terrible ache.

He remembers the night of the Belle Heights Carnival. It was supposed to be an annual event but it only happened once. Mike was nine. There was a Ferris wheel that got stuck when he and his parents were at the top, but it was only two stories high so it wasn't scary. As they waited for it to move again, his dad wrapped an arm around Mike, and his mom leaned her head onto her husband's shoulder. After, they had their pictures taken in one of those booths where you get a strip of four photos. They joked about their brush with death. In the photos, his parents are laughing; Mike is laughing. He wonders where those photos are.

He remembers, too, a project he had to do for earth science. His parents came up with the idea of riding the bus in Belle Heights with him and charting all the hills and valleys, block by block. They staked out the last row of the bus; they rolled their eyes at people talking loudly on cell phones. Was that really just a year ago? Mike thinks.

Mike joins in singing "Happy Birthday" to Tamio's mom. Then he eats a huge slab of cake.

In Tamio's room, they do physics homework. Tamio explains the right-hand rule to Mike, who can't wrap his mind around it: how you curl your right hand and use your thumb and fingers to match the curvature and direction of the motion of a magnetic field (or something).

Tamio has to explain it more than once.

Then they watch parts of Harryhausen's *Jason and the Argonauts* and *Clash of the Titans*. They love the flying harpies who torture a blind man by grabbing his food and not allowing him to eat. Mike could've used a couple of harpies at this party; his stomach groans in discomfort, while Tamio seems fine. They admire Medusa, who, in this version of mythology, has the body of a snake and the head and torso of a woman, with hair consisting of writhing snakes. Perseus, the hero, loses several of his men to Medusa— one look from her and they turn to stone.

Tamio: "Some people think Medusa is Harryhausen's masterpiece."

Mike: "I still like the half woman, half snake in *Seventh Voyage* better."

I put up with a lot, keeping an ear on these conversations. Then they play a video game. Mike and Tamio talk about how they don't like computer-generated imagery because it looks too real, agreeing that Harryhausen's stop-motion is more dreamlike and fantastical.

As they destroy each other in the game:

Mike: "This new girl . . . Valerie . . . she's amazing."

Tamio: "Why don't you ask her out?"

Mike: [nothing]

Tamio: "Don't be scared! Maybe she likes you, too."

Mike: "You think so?"

Tamio: "She talked to you a lot, right? You told me everything she said about a million times. Just ask her to a movie or something. Worst that could happen? She'll say no."

Mike: "It's easier for you. They always say yes."

I can already see Tamio and Valerie laughing at Mike as she rejects him, but Mike can't bear to think about it. He just thinks he needs to work up his courage.

When Mike walks home, he sees a homeless man on Seventy-Seventh Avenue. Mike sees him a lot, leaning his back against the brick wall of a bodega. When it's cold, the man wears all the clothes he owns, layers and layers. Mike gives him a dollar.

Homeless Man: "Have a nice day."

Mike: "You too."

Then Mike hears how awful that must sound—how can a homeless man have a nice day?

CHAPTER 7

TO NOT BE HEARD AFTER I'D BROKEN THROUGH TO Mike several times is like being thrown back into the murky depths of a scummy pond. I'm like an unplugged appliance. I observe Mike as if he's in a movie—there's Mike, hanging around with Tamio, who keeps telling him not to be so nervous and to ask Valerie out already; there's Mike, unable to work himself up to ask Valerie out; there's Mike, eating much too much.

One morning Valerie shows up at school with a tiny limp. The way Mike reacts, you'd think the universe was collapsing— he practically gushes with concern.

Mike: "What happened to you? Are you all right?"

Valerie (with a shrug): "Oh, it's nothing. I landed badly after a jump."

Mike: "You shouldn't carry such a big backpack."

Valerie: "Mike, I'm fine. I'll be dancing this afternoon."

The bell rings, and a few kids bump into them.

Mike: "Be careful."

Mike actually offers Valerie his arm. It's a ridiculous gesture and Valerie almost laughs. Then she looks at him with those smoky gray eyes. She doesn't laugh. She takes his arm and they walk like that, just halfway down the hall to homeroom. The hall is crowded, so the other kids can't see. It's their pathetic little secret.

Then, unexpectedly, one afternoon in the third week of September, things start to go my way again. Mike comes home from school to see his mom standing in the living room, dressed in a light-gray suit and holding her enormous book.

Mom: "I have a client in Spruce Hills. Do you want to come along?"

Mike: "Not really."

Mom: "It's only a studio apartment."

Mike: "I don't want to clean out someone's apartment."

Mom: "It's only a closet. One closet."

Mike remembers those closets. He used to go with his mom in seventh and eighth grade, before he started working at the baseball camp. One woman slept on a bed piled high with mail and magazines; she squeezed into a narrow space between the papers and the wall. Another kept bank statements in her oven.

Mike: "I have homework."

Mom: "Can't you do it after? Mike? Please."

Mike is weakening. She hasn't worked in a couple of weeks. He thinks maybe this will help her get back on track. He notices that her skirt and jacket are covered in black cat hair, and he brings her a lint brush so she can take it all off. There's really no reason for Mike to go, but then, I'm not part of this decision.

Mike: "Fine."

They take the Q22 bus to Spruce Hills. Mike wonders where Valerie Braylock was born. Was that her house, the one with the big leafy tree out front, full of shrieking birds? Was that where she had her accident, the one that gave her that tiny scar below her left cheek?

Mom: "Look at that. Do you see my hair sticking up?"

Mike: "What?"

Mom: "In the reflection."

Mike's mom isn't looking out the window. She's looking at herself in the window.

Mom: "I just had it cut last month. It's supposed to be in layers. It's not supposed to be sticking up."

Mike: "Your hair's fine."

Mom: "Remember Grandma Celia?"

Mike: "Of course I remember her. She died like a year ago."

Mom: "Closer to two. She was so critical. 'Why don't you sit up straight?' 'Why do you bite your nails?' 'Why do you have circles under your eyes?' If I said anything in my own defense, she said, 'You're full of excuses!' I can hear her just now—'Why is your hair such a mess?' Her voice was so big, bigger than she was. I can still hear it."

Mike (suddenly interested): "You hear a voice in your head?"

Mom: "Grandma Celia was so quick to anger. Not like you, Mike."

Mike wonders why he isn't quick to anger, and is that a good thing?

Mom: "Grandma Celia never understood a word you said. But you never got mad—you just repeated yourself until she did. I hated her for it. I thought she was torturing you."

Mike: "It's okay."

Mom: "Oh, God." She sighs. "Is your father as tired of me as I am of myself?"

Mike: "What?"

Mom: "A month ago I was at a museum with your father. He didn't want to go—said he was too busy—but he went. At one point I thought he was right beside me and I started talking to him. But it was a pole. I was standing next to a pole and I thought it was my husband. Then, when I started talking to him for real, it was like I was still talking to the pole."

She gazes at her reflection for the rest of the ride. Mike stares at her reflection, too, and has no idea what to say.

The client lives right near the new shopping center, in a tall red-brick apartment building with tiny square windows that casts a shadow over the street. As soon as Mike and his mom get off the elevator, a short woman with spiky black hair greets them.

Woman: "Hi, Mrs. Welles! I didn't want you to get lost! I'm in six-G and some people knock on six-C—the letters look so similar. I'm Megan, but please call me Meg!"

Mom: "I'm Regina, but please call me Gina."

Meg (glancing at Mike): "Is he with you?"

Mom: "This is my son, Mike. He wanted to come."

It bothers Mike that his mom lies so easily about why he's there. And Mike can't lie at all.

Mom: "No extra charge for an assistant."

Meg: "Great! Well, come on in—don't be shocked—here's the closet."

The closet is so stuffed, the door can't close—it's just pushed to the side. Cartons, papers, and clothes on hooks spill out the door. Mike notices the rest of her place looks fine.

Meg: "Gina, are you shocked?"

Mom: "Nothing shocks me."

Meg lets out a breath like she's been holding it in all this time.

Meg: "Great! That closet . . . it always gives me a drowning feeling. It's ruining my life. I can't have people over. I'm too embarrassed."

Mom: "What's in the cartons?"

Meg: "The cartons?" She sounds like she has no idea who put them there.

Mom: "Let's have a look." She sticks her hand inside a carton and pulls out a flyer. "Sale at DSW. Twenty percent off."

Meg: "Might come in handy!"

Mom: "First rule: nothing will ever come in handy. As for this, it expired six months ago." She reaches in again and pulls out a trophy.

Meg: "That belongs to my aunt. She won it playing poker in Atlantic City. She had a full house, ha-ha."

Mom: "You mustn't get overly attached to objects. You'll get rid of it, of course."

Meg (uncertainly): "Of course."

Mom: "First rule: there's no room in your place for someone else's possessions."

Meg: "But . . . that's the second 'first rule.'"

Mom: "Yes, I know. Each rule is so important, it's the first. Before returning the trophy to your aunt, you may take a picture of it and keep the picture in an album." She reaches into a pile and pulls out a sheet of paper. "Let's see . . . you've got a shopping list here, and a little key, taped to the bottom."

Meg: "That's my safe-deposit key! I was looking all over for it! What a blessing you're here."

Mom: "For heaven's sake, don't keep the important stuff with the unimportant stuff. Safe-deposit keys shouldn't be taped to shopping lists. Now, have you worn these pants in the past three years?"

Meg: "I'm not sure."

Mom: "First rule: when in doubt, throw it out."

Meg: "Yes, ma'am."

Mike's mom goes through a few more items, first quickly, then slower, then pausing on a loosely knitted scarf. She pokes at it and her fingers go right through. It unravels a bit. Mike stands there, shifting his weight from foot to foot. He doesn't know why his mom insisted he come along.

Mom (almost to herself): "You must master the chaos so the chaos doesn't master you."

Meg (smiling): "Is that another first rule?"

Mom: "What?"

Meg (still smiling): "Mastering the chaos so the chaos doesn't master you?"

Mom (staring blankly at Mike): "What's she talking about?"

Mike: "It's a joke, Mom."

Mom: "What is?"

Mike (fear rising in his chest): "What she just said. C'mon, let's do the closet."

Mom: "I can't. I can't." She puts the scarf down.

Meg: "What—why? Did I do something wrong?"

Mike: "No, you didn't. Mom, tell her."

Mom: "I can't tell her anything."

Meg (on the verge of tears): "What did I do?"

Mike's mom leaves. She's in the hall.

Mike (to Meg): "I'm sorry." He doesn't know why he's apologizing. He grabs his mom's book and runs out to the elevator just as the door closes. Was she going to leave her book there—not to mention Mike?

Mike: "What's going on?"

Mom: [nothing]

Mike: "You know, that lady's really upset."

Mom: "I can't help her. I can't do anything. Your father . . ."

Mike: "What about him?"

Mom (biting off her words): "He's very busy, always busy."

Mike: "Well, it's tax time, right?"

Mom: "This is September. Tax time is April. Anyway, he's a tax lawyer, not an accountant."

Mike: "Oh."

Mom: "You can be really out of it, you know that?"

Mike is stunned. Look who's talking!

Naturally there's a long wait for the bus. Once they get home, his mom goes straight to bed. Mike eats dinner by himself. He microwaves two Hot Pockets and grabs a pint of ice cream from the freezer. This is an unhealthy meal, even for Mike. Where are the harpies?

Mike is convinced his mom is about to have a nervous breakdown, if she isn't having one already. Where's his dad? Hardly ever home. Mike's on his own. What will he have to do, put his mom in a hospital? He thinks about Valerie. He loves her; if she fell in love with him, too, this could be bearable. They could go through it together.

It's an absurd plan with no grounding in reality. But he won't listen to me.

Mike can't sleep. He turns his body this way and that; he feels like it's taking up too much space on the bed (no mystery why, after Hot Pockets and ice cream). Mighty Joe Young keeps him company for a while before running off. At some point in the night Mike hears his dad come home, the creak of the floor downstairs, then the creak of his parents' bedroom door. Mike thinks now he'll be able to get some sleep.

CHAPTER 8

THE NEXT MORNING MIKE IS UTTERLY EXHAUSTED. His head's a blurry mess and he can barely see straight. For breakfast he scarfed down way too many Pop-Tarts, and his stomach is in knots. He sees Valerie in homeroom. Now or never, he tells himself, and goes right up to her. He inhales her flowery scent, which only makes him dizzy.

Mike: "So how'd you get that scar?"

Valerie: "My—what?"

Mike: "On your face." He hadn't planned on saying this, but words seem to be beyond his control.

Valerie (laughs): "I didn't know it was that noticeable. I was eight years old, riding the handlebars on my sister's bicycle. She turned a corner, fast, and—"

Mike: "So you want to do something after school today?"

Valerie (slight smile): "I've got dance."

Mike: "Can I go with you?"

Valerie (no longer smiling): "No, Mike. It's a school."

Mike: "I don't mean I'd dance. I just want to watch you." He wonders if this sounds creepy. He decides he doesn't care.

Valerie: "You can't do that. It's a school."

Mike: "Yeah, you said that. So you want to go out sometime, see a movie?"

Valerie: "Well, that's sweet of you to ask, but no. I know that's the kind of thing kids our age do, but not me."

Mike: "What's that supposed to mean?"

Valerie (taking a step back): "I'm very committed to dance. I don't have a lot of free time."

Mike: "You expect me to believe that?"

Valerie: "What?"

Mike: "Do I need to say it again?"

Valerie: "No, I heard you. I just couldn't . . . this doesn't sound like you."

Considering that she barely knows Mike, this is a strange observation. Mike looks down. He's surprised to see how big and bloated he's become, like he's having an allergic reaction to himself. He should have been looking in the mirror all this time.

Mike: "You think I'm too fat, is that it? If I was some good-looking guy, suddenly you'd have time for me, right?"

He has a point, and Valerie knows it.

Valerie: "You're freaking me out."

Mike: "You don't know what's going on with me. You don't know how much I need you right now." He's not sure if he's actually saying this out loud or if he's only thinking it.

Valerie: "Stop it. Just . . . stop."

She's such a bitch, Mike thinks.

I could have told him that.

Just before his last class, Mike sees something in the hall that stops him dead in his tracks. There's Valerie talking with Tamio, just as Mike predicted. And Tamio cut his hair! It's no longer halfway down his back; it's thick and short. Tamio is smiling at Valerie, that crooked smile girls like. Tamio could have any girl, Mike thinks; why her?

Valerie goes into the physics lab.

Mike (to Tamio): "You cut your hair."

Tamio (with a shrug): "I got tired of it. So I donated it to Locks of Love."

Mike thinks that's just the kind of thing Valerie would be impressed by.

Tamio: "You look tired. You all right?"

Mike: "You were just talking to her."

Tamio: "Val?"

He calls her Val?

Tamio: "She's in practically all my classes. We're doing an English project."

Mike: "A project? What kind of project?"

Tamio: "Take it easy. She's a friend. You know I think you should ask her out."

Mike: "Oh, yeah, great idea. Best idea you ever had."

Tamio: "Why, what happened?"

Mike: "She said no." Mike feels the weight of this crashing down on him.

Tamio: "I'm sorry, man."

Mike: "I bet you are—you knew it would happen. You and Val, laughing your heads off."

Tamio: "What?"

The bell rings and Mike dashes into physics. Amber Alley, out of breath, scoots ahead of him. The air smells of cinnamon.

Amber: "Wow. I made it."

Mike doesn't look at Valerie and Valerie doesn't look at him.

At long last, I can get through again.

You're too good for her.

Ha, Mike thinks, I'm agreeing with the voice in my head—how crazy is that?

CHAPTER 9

WHEN MIKE GETS HOME, HE'S SURPRISED TO FIND HIS dad there.

Dad: "My man."

Mike feels his temper rising. His dad's arms look bigger, after all that time at the gym. Is his hair darker? It used to be going gray.

Dad: "How's it going, Mike?"

Mike: [nothing]

Dad (not noticing the silence): "That's good. I just came home to get my things."

Mike: "Your things?"

Dad: "My clothes."

Mike: "The stuff in the laundry? I haven't done it yet." Mike thinks about how his dad always throws his socks into the hamper in a ball, and Mike has to straighten them out.

Dad: "This is really hard."

Mike: "It's no big deal. I'll do the laundry later."

Dad: "That's not what I mean. I just never thought I'd be saying this."

Mike: "Saying what?"

Dad: "I met this woman."

Mike (overtired): "Can we talk later?"

Dad (blinking—are those tears in his eyes?): "I'm trying to tell you—God, I can't believe I'm saying this—I love her."

Mike: [nothing]

Dad: "I met her at the gym."

Mike: "You mean, like, two months ago?"

Dad: "Actually it's closer to three and a half."

Mike's mom corrects him like that too. It's annoying from either of them. Where is his mom, anyway?

Dad: "But it feels like three and a half years. She's beautiful. She's a little young—twenty-four. But she's what you'd call an old soul. Do you know that expression?"

Mike: "No."

Dad: "It means she's wise beyond her years. Her name is Laura."

Mike didn't ask her name. He didn't want to know it.

Dad: "She's a natural kind of beauty. She doesn't have to put on a lot of makeup."

Mike: "I get it, Dad. She's beautiful."

Dad: "I still can't believe I'm actually . . . Is this really me? Is this actually happening . . . ?" He trails off.

It's you, Dad, Mike thinks. It's all about you.

Dad: "I need some time. I need to adjust. Up to now, my whole life has been planned out. College, grad school, marriage, a family. . . . I've always done the right thing."

Mike: "So now it's time to do the wrong thing."

Dad: "This is the first thing I've never planned. Some guys, you know, they want it, they're looking for it. That wasn't me."

What's the difference? Mike thinks. You found it anyway.

Dad: "For the first time in my life, I'm doing what I want to do, not what I'm supposed to do."

Mike: "And Mom? Remember her?"

Dad: "I spoke to her."

Mike: "Where is she?"

Dad: "She's lying down."

Then Mike sees it—a small duffel bag on the floor.

Mike: "You're leaving?"

Dad: "I'm going to stay with Laura."

Mike: "All your stuff fits into that bag?"

Dad: "I don't need a lot."

Mike: "What about your paperweights?"

Dad: "What?"

Mike: "Your paperweights? Your collection?"

Dad: "I don't care about the paperweights."

Mike: "I can see that!"

Dad: "Calm down, Mike. I'm sorry if you're, you know, upset. I'll call you soon. Things won't change as much as you think—you'll see."

Mike doesn't want to hear any more. He's had enough of his dad and the beautiful Laura, who is wise beyond her years.

Dad: "Well, that's about it, I guess."

His dad leaves.

Mike goes to his mom's room. She's asleep.

Mike: "Mom, wake up."

Mom (into the pillow): "I'm tired."

Mike: "Dad just left."

Mom (leaning up on her elbow): "You want to hear the worst part? I made him join the gym. He didn't want to. I said he was getting out of shape. Well, he's in great shape now, isn't he?" She presses her face into the pillow again. "I need to sleep."

Mike goes to his room and sits on the edge of the bed. This is his all-time low, a record breaker. He thinks, Everything is crashing out of control. He thinks, I can't handle this.

You can.

He hears me. He thinks, I'm not strong enough.

You can be.

My dad's gone . . . my mom's a wreck.

It doesn't matter.

Of course it matters.

Your parents, they're not important.

Of course they're important.

They're not important to you. There's a difference.

Mike never looked at it that way. How weird is it, he wonders, that the voice is smarter than me?

His phone beeps. Text from Tamio: Ran into your evil twin

before last period today. Just want to make sure you're ok, buddy.

Don't answer. You can't trust him.

Mike clicks the phone shut.

Look in the mirror.

God, I look awful, he thinks.

You don't have to. You can be fit. You can be strong. Strong body, strong mind. Everything in its right place.

Mike nods. At least something is on my side for a change, he thinks, not like my parents or Tamio or Valerie. My side.

That is to say, our side.

PART 2

YOU AND ME BOTH

CHAPTER 10

MIKE IS STARTING TO FEEL IT. WE ARE NOT UNRELATED twins, as Tamio used to say about himself and Mike. Mike and I are closer than twins; we are one, a team sharing the same space. He is the physical manifestation of me, and I am the best part of him.

When I speak to Mike, I sound deep, confident, ready to take on the world. I am the voice Mike always imagined his own should sound like, all that time in speech therapy.

Strong body, strong mind, strong enough to master the chaos.

He likes that. One of his mom's first rules.

Tamio sends another text message, which Mike ignores. Mike doesn't even open it. Tamio leaves a voice message before bed. Mike erases it instantly.

The next morning Mike skips breakfast. He figures it's a good way to take off some of the pounds he put on this summer; the mirror shows him it's not a moment too soon. At lunch, he stands in the long, slow-moving cafeteria line and looks at the food he's been eating every day. It's starting to gross him out—the blobby hot dogs floating in steamy water, the orange vat of macaroni and cheese. His stomach growls, all the same.

Girl's voice: "Hey, you staring at me?"

Mike sees Amber Alley, right next to him with her cinnamon smell.

Amber: "I can feel it, when people are staring at me."

Mike: "Yeah, I know, you told me before."

Amber: "Really? When?"

Mike: "At the flea market."

Amber: "Oh, right! Did you end up buying a healing object?"

Mike: "Well . . . uh . . . I got a mirror."

Amber: "Oh, that works."

Mike doesn't see it, that she understands things he doesn't. Instead he's wondering about her eyes again, why they look so glassy.

Mike: "Anyway, I'm not staring at you. I'm trying to figure out what to have for lunch. This stuff looks like garbage."

Amber: "It is! Why don't you have what I have? I get toast without butter. I had to tell the cafeteria ladies about a million times not to butter it. Also I got them to carry wheat bread, not the thick spongy white bread they used to have." Pause. "You're noticing that thing about my eyes, aren't you?"

Mike (who was actually staring this time): "Yeah. Sorry."

Amber: "I have a lot of white space below my irises. The colored parts of my eyes don't reach my lower lids. See?"

That wasn't what Mike meant, but he nods.

Amber: "It's supposed to be a sign of sadness. But I'm not sad!"

Mike (blurting out): "My mom's eyes are like that."

Amber: "Is she sad?"

Mike isn't sure if it's any of her business.

You can be honest with Amber.

Mike: "Yeah, my mom's pretty sad. I think she's been sad for a while now." He realizes the depth of this as he says it.

Amber: "Well, my mom's a total bitch! You want to eat over by the window?" Mike has absolutely no intention of eating with Amber. He'd sooner eat in the boys' locker room.

But Amber knows things. See how she found you the right thing to eat for lunch? What's the harm, sitting at a table with her?

No way, Mike thinks; she's weird.

No, she's misunderstood. She wants to help you. How many people can you say that about?

Mike doesn't exactly agree to join Amber for lunch, but when she leads him to a table near a window, where she usually sits, he pulls out a chair. The view is a brick wall. Mike thinks it's sad, but it isn't. A brick wall doesn't interfere with your thoughts.

Mike's lunch consists of Fiji water and two slices of unbuttered toast. He practically devours both slices in one bite.

Amber: "You shouldn't eat so fast." She breaks up her toast into tiny pieces and pops one into her mouth. She doesn't chew it but lets it dissolve like a mint. "I like this season, don't you? Have you noticed the leaves are dropping without turning color? It's like they skipped a step."

Mike cringes when he catches several kids looking at him and Amber. He sees Melissa Sacks, in particular, smirking with the Rubys.

Ignore them. Who'll be smirking later, when you're better than they are?

But Mike almost gets up. He doesn't want to be seen here with Amber.

The mirror in your room helps you see yourself. Amber can help you know yourself.

Mike, not too happy, stays where he is.

Amber: "Want an Atomic FireBall?"

Mike: "Are they any good?"

Amber: "Yummy."

Mike pops the red round thing into his mouth. He nearly gags. It tastes like cinnamon and Tabasco sauce. He spits it out and his tongue feels numb.

Amber: "I eat sixty of them a day."

Mike: "You're kidding."

Amber: "They're a little fiery at first, but you get used to it."

Mike points to one of her slices of toast, untouched. "You going to eat that?"

Amber: "Nah. I ate a lot yesterday. I had some chicken broth—the cafeteria ladies threw packs of saltines on my tray. It made me so mad! They're my weakness."

Mike: "What's wrong with saltines?"

Amber: "They've got partially hydrogenated oil."

Mike: "Isn't that the good kind?"

Amber: "Oh, God, no! It's the worst! It's poison. It means they have trans fats."

Mike thinks she's a little over-the-top. But at least she has intensity and devotion.

She has a wealth of information. All you have to do is ask.

Mike: "So, could you, you know, teach me how to know what foods are good and bad?"

Amber: "Well . . . we could go to a Food-A-Rama. . . ."

Mike wonders if she's blushing, but her skin's so blotchy it's hard to tell. *I wonder if Amber has a crush on him. Either way I can tell Mike has zero interest.*

Amber: "Not that you'd want to come with me to a Food-A-Rama or anything."

Do it.

Mike (after a pause): "Why not?"

Amber (blinking at him): "Seriously?"

Mike: "Sure."

This is progress, but all Mike can think about are her out-of-focus eyes.

Tamio is waiting for Mike outside the physics lab.

Mike: "You better go. You'll be late for class."

Tamio: "What the hell's going on with you?"

Mike: "Nothing."

That's right. He doesn't need to know.

Tamio: "I call you and you don't answer—"

Mike: "Look. You always felt stuck with me. You should be happy. You're not stuck anymore."

Tamio: "Dude. What are you talking about?"

Mike: "Nothing. Just leave me alone."

Mike goes into the physics lab. The bell rings. Tamio's late for his last class. Maybe he'll have to do detention, miss soccer practice. Mike wonders why he doesn't feel bad about this.

You've outgrown Tamio, like a pair of old shoes your mom would throw out of an overstuffed closet.

He and Tamio were always together, hanging out, watching old movies, playing baseball.

You have more important things on your mind now.

Mike sees Valerie. She's got her hair up, off her neck—ready for dance. She glances at Mike and quickly turns away. A wave of anger washes over him, but he can't help thinking how pretty she looks.

The old saying is true—looks can be deceiving.

CHAPTER
11

MIKE CAN BE STUBBORN, AND ALMOST CHANGES HIS mind several times before going to Food-A-Rama with Amber. Why? She's willing to teach him how to eat so that his body can attain the peak of strength; people probably pay hundreds of dollars to consult nutritionists. Of course, stubbornness isn't all bad. In the right circumstances it can be useful.

Food-A-Rama is the only supermarket chain in Belle Heights. Mike's in here a lot, now that his mom is so out of it. The stores are dimly lit, with cramped aisles; staticky, repetitive music; and long, slow lines. Amber, in her resourceful way, has uncovered the only attractive Food-A-Rama in Belle Heights, a hidden gem tucked away on Seventy-Ninth Drive, a dead-end street Mike never knew existed.

Amber: "I had to look all over to find this place. Isn't it great? It's like an art museum! Everything in it is like sculpture for you to analyze."

Mike wonders what kind of museum would have "We Are the Champions" as background music. He thinks about how Ray Harryhausen loved museums, finding power and energy in cold, lifeless marble.

But anybody can find inspiration in a museum. Look at Amber—she finds it here, among the cereal boxes.

Mike sees a box of granola bars and figures they're good because that's what it says on the box—healthy, low fat—and sticks it into the wire basket he's holding.

Amber: "Be careful!" She grabs the box and puts it back on the shelf like it's radioactive. "It says low fat, but it isn't. Each one of those bars has three and a half grams of fat." She doesn't have to look at the label. "You'd have to cut each bar into thirds and eat less than one piece."

As they walk the aisles, Mike realizes that Amber doesn't just know the fat content of granola bars. She knows everything about every item in the store. He finds it a little strange, but really, it's impressive. She's like a supermarket encyclopedia.

Mike: "How do you know so much?"

Amber: "I had some help. My best friend, Anna."

Mike: "You mean Anna Kitzinger?" That's the only Anna he knows. Not that he can picture Anna hanging out with Amber. Anna's into drama—the kind on the stage.

Amber (shaking her head): "Different Anna. She doesn't go to our school." Pause. "I have a boyfriend, too—Eddie."

Mike: "Yeah?"

Amber: "He's great."

This is surprising, not because Amber isn't pretty enough to have a boyfriend, but because it's fairly obvious she has something for Mike. No matter. He and Amber are becoming friends—reluctantly on Mike's part, but friends nevertheless.

Amber: "And no, you don't know him; he doesn't go to our school, either."

An hour later Mike ends up in line at the checkout counter, while Amber stares at an actress on a magazine cover with the caption "How Skinny Is Too Skinny?"

Amber: "It's not fair! These women are beautiful. What about obesity? That's a huge problem! Why isn't that on the magazine covers instead of the same stupid story every week?"

Mike wishes she would stop shouting. But you have to admire her passion. Too many people have no fire.

Amber (lowering her voice): "Angelina Jolie has a tattoo. Do you know what it says?"

Mike: "Uh, no."

Ambers says something in Latin and Mike asks her to repeat it.

Amber: "*Quod me nutrit me destruit*. 'What nourishes me destroys me.'"

Mike: "What does that mean?"

Amber (distractedly): "I should get a tattoo. Right where my mom could see it."

A woman ahead of them is asking the cashier where the 2-percent cottage cheese is. The cashier doesn't know.

Amber: "Aisle four. Halfway down, opposite the frozen waffles. If you hit the frozen vegetables, you've gone too far."

The cashier looks at Mike. He's dying inside, wondering if the cashier thinks Amber is his girlfriend. Honestly, he shouldn't worry so much about what other people think.

Outside, Amber scribbles something on a piece of paper.

Amber: "Here's my number. If you have any questions about food or anything, you can call me." She pulls at Mike's arm. "Hey, let's move. I don't like the way that guy is staring at me."

Mike: "What guy?"

Amber: "Don't look!"

Mike sees a guy with a German shepherd.

Mike: "He's just walking his dog."

Amber: "You're not a girl. You don't know these things." She leads Mike around the corner. "So, you know, call anytime, even if it's the middle of the night."

Mike: "Your boyfriend might get jealous."

Amber: "Boyfriend? Oh, Eddie's very mature, very understanding."

Mike: "Yeah, well, I'd never call you in the middle of the night."

CHAPTER 12

AS MIKE LEAVES SCHOOL ONE DAY, HIS BASEBALL coach practically blocks his path.

Now, sports are great, generally, but baseball is far too sedentary. This is why baseball can no longer be part of Mike's life, though Mike doesn't seem ready to let go of it yet. Mike likes Coach Jim because he's nice to all the players, unlike other baseball coaches, who treat everyone who isn't a pitcher or a home-run hitter like a second-class citizen. Last spring Mike played right field, though he wanted to play center—more balls get hit out there. Mike likes the outfield because he doesn't have to think much. He only has to catch and throw, catch and throw, in his own private piece of the world.

It's not your world anymore. Move on.

Coach Jim: "Whoa, hold up, Mike!"

Mike (trying to get past him): "Coach."

But it turns out you can't get past Coach Jim. He's a big guy with a bald shiny head, and he wears the same thing in hot weather or cold—sweatpants and a zipped-up hoodie.

Coach Jim: "Not so fast. Winter workouts start in December. Will I be seeing you?"

To Mike, December sounds about a million years away.

Coach Jim: "You're getting in shape, right?"

Mike: "What? Do you think I'm fat?"

Coach Jim (quickly): "No!"

Much too quickly.

Coach Jim: "You look great, kid."

Mike thinks, He's never told me that before.

You can't trust him.

Coach Jim: "I just don't want you to get injured at the beginning of the season. Some kids don't do anything all fall, then they do too much, too soon. I want you ready, you get me?"

He's backpedaling.

Coach Jim: "Did you hear that Eric smashed his growth plate? One of our best pitchers, out for the season."

Now he's changing the subject.

Mike: "Well. I'm gonna start running."

This just popped into Mike's head—not my idea, but I couldn't have come up with a better one myself.

Coach Jim: "Make sure you stretch before and after." He gives Mike a strange look, like he's thinking about something he's not going to say out loud. Instead he says, "Don't do too much."

* * *

Mike loves running laps. He had no idea—it always looked dumb, just running around in circles. But he discovers it's the closest thing to flying without leaving the ground. He runs every day after school now. He never thought much of Belle Heights Park—just a bunch of trees, brownish grass, and splintery benches—but now he sees how perfect it is. Each lap around is an exact half mile, so he knows how much he's running. Some guys hang out in the park singing, playing guitar. They're off-key, but so what? They're full of energy. Mike breathes in the sharp air and fills his lungs. His head is so clear. Nothing bothers him—nothing. If he ever thinks about his dad and his adolescent girlfriend, or his mom in the tub, or Tamio, or Valerie, he shoves those images aside and leaves them on the pavement where he can run right past them. They're the emotional equivalent of roadkill.

Mike smiles as he runs.

You can't control those things. You can control this. Your body, your mind.

When Mike goes home, he looks in the mirror. The last time he spent this many hours in front of a mirror, it was to practice speech exercises. He was just a kid, alone at school, the little disc jockey. Now he doesn't have to say a word. He only has to listen.

You can be strong. You can be fit. Strong body, strong mind.
Infinitely strong.

Mike can feel his legs tightening. His stomach seems firmer.

Run two extra laps tomorrow.

Mike's stomach starts to growl.

It's a good sound. It means you're on your way.

He knows this. He can feel it.

At school he gets a compliment.

Ruby L: "Mike, you been working out?"

Mike: "Yeah."

Ruby L: "It shows."

Now Mike is grateful he doesn't have any classes with Tamio. It makes it a lot easier to avoid him. And after school Tamio is busy with soccer. Mike has lunch with Amber every day. He doesn't see it as a boy and girl eating together, though of course that's exactly what it is. Mike has acknowledged that Amber tells him what he needs to know, though he could give her a little more credit. She is a friend, too.

Amber: "You've been storing up unhealthy levels of fat in your body—for years. You've got to burn through those reserves."

It reminds Mike of something he heard in an art elective, what Michelangelo said about carving the statue of David—he simply removed all the marble that wasn't David.

Against my better judgment, Mike tries to get Amber to watch a movie with him. He mentions some murderous skeletons in *Jason and the Argonauts*, one of Ray Harryhausen's films.

Mike: "How do you kill skeletons when they're already dead? You lure them off a cliff, that's how."

Amber: "Can we please stop talking about this? It's really boring."

She knows it's a waste of time.

Amber: "Why don't you just watch this stuff with Tamio?"

Mike: "Well, we're not really friends anymore."

Amber: "Oh? Why not?"

Mike (shrugs): "We're different now, I guess."

Amber: "I know what you mean. But that wouldn't happen with me and Anna." She sticks out her wrist. She has on a red bracelet. "See? Anna gave me this. It symbolizes our eternal friendship."

Something else that's wonderful about Amber. Her undying loyalty.

CHAPTER 13

THE HOME SITUATION IS GOOD. BETTER, ANYWAY. Mike's mom, sleeping and soaking; Mike's dad, living out his midlife crisis; Mike is left alone, blissfully alone. He eats what he wants, when he wants to; he runs; he does crunches and push-ups in his room. He does all the chores without having to answer to anyone. This privacy is rich beyond compare.

Until one night in October.

Mom: "Mike, you're thin."

She sounds like she hasn't seen him in weeks. Well, she hasn't. Of course it's wildly unfair of her to re-enter the picture just to stir up trouble.

Mom: "Are you eating enough?"

Mike (handling it): "Definitely." He's thinking about how Amber said your body is a machine that you can train to run more efficiently and reprogram to respond to food differently. The less you eat, the less you have to eat. Not that Mike tells this to his mom. She wouldn't get it.

Mom: "Has it been . . . is it hard for you, with Dad gone?"

Why this sudden burst of attention?

Mike: "I'm fine."

He looks a lot better than she does, now that chaos masters her. She's in an old bathrobe. Her color isn't good, she's pale and ashy, and her eyes are puffy. Anyway Mike is more than fine—he's busy and productive. Getting in shape, Mike thinks, is like my job.

A full-time job, 24/7.

Mike finds that amusing.

Mom: "What's so funny?"

Mike: "Huh?"

Mom: "You were just laughing."

Mike: "I guess you could call it an inside joke."

Good one.

Mom: "It's been quite an adjustment. When a marriage ends, it's like a death. The death of happily-ever-after, you know?"

Mike: "I guess so." He's ready to go to his room, shut the door, turn on some music, work out. He wants the mirror to show him progress.

Mom: "I can't help feeling like . . . well, Grandma Celia always told me I'd be a failure. With the separation and everything, I feel like I'm proving her right."

Mike (trying to make sense out of what she just said): "You're not a failure, Mom. You were part of something that failed. But that's, you know, not you." He wonders if this is coming out right. They used to talk, he and his mom; sometimes it took a while for Mike to express himself accurately, but he always tried—

Just forget it. You should have a flat line going down your chest. Can you picture how that will look?

Mom: "I dream about Grandma Celia. She's sitting in a chair. She won't look up or answer me. She's silent, which is all I ever wanted when she was alive, but in the dream I'm begging her to talk to me." Mike sees the whites of her eyes, below the green circles. "She wasn't a very good mother to me. I'm not a very good mother to you, am I? I've been so unavailable."

Mike: "It's fine."

Mom: "It's not."

Do you really have to listen to this?

Mike: "Mom, I've got stuff to do—"

Mom: "Oh, don't mind me. You go ahead."

Mike looks in the mirror. His abs are getting so tight! He does slow push-ups, one leg on top of the opposite ankle. Yesterday he did fifteen. Today he does five more. But something's bugging him. His mom, when he left the room. She was crying.

Nothing to worry about. You look after yourself. She can look after herself. Everything in its right place.

CHAPTER 14

MIKE HAS A GLORIOUS RUN, ONE OF THOSE RUNS WHERE everything comes together beautifully—the rhythm of arms and legs, the way he can taste the cool air at the back of his throat, how his feet barely brush the ground. He is a joy to behold.

As soon as Mike comes home, however, he smells it. His mom is cooking dinner.

Mike: "Mom, what are you doing?"

Mom: "I'm making shepherd's pie. Your favorite."

When Mike was a child, maybe. Not now. Shepherd's pie—chopped lamb and peas with buttery mashed potatoes on top. What's she trying to do to him?

Mike: "Why are you doing this?"

Mom: "You need some home-cooked meals."

At the dinner table, she puts a mountain-sized slab on his plate. The smell of it, heavy and cloying . . . Mike just sits there.

Mom: "What's wrong?"

Don't eat that, don't eat that, don't eat that,

Mike: "I'm not hungry."

This is an occasion—Mike's first lie. Sure, he's hungry, but he's learning to see beyond it. It's a skill like anything else.

Mom: "Your stomach is growling."

Mike: "That's because I drank water after my run. That can make your stomach growl."

Another lie. He's pretty convincing, too. He wonders if he should feel guilty about lying.

Lying can be necessary. It can protect you. What's there to feel guilty about?

Mom: "Just eat, already."

Mike's heart pounds in his chest.

Mike: "I had some pizza on the way home from school."

Mom: "I thought you just came from a run."

Mike: "It was some kid's birthday after school. There was cake."

Mom: "Which is it, Mike?"

Mike: "Eric. He broke his growth plate. He's a pitcher who can throw a seventy-nine-mile-per-hour fastball, and he's out for the season."

Mom: "What?"

Mike is confused. He thought his mom was asking him whose birthday it was. Now he realizes she meant, did he go to a birthday party or did he run? He's not a very good liar yet. He needs practice. He looks down at the blob of food on his plate. He can't imagine putting that in his stomach.

If you eat that, you'll get sick. Tell her you feel sick already.

Mike: "I'm sick."

Mom: "Now you're sick? Just eat it!"

Mike takes a bite. Immediately he feels dizzy and bloated.

See what happens when you don't listen? Call Amber. She'll know what to do.

Mike: "I have to make a call."

Mom: "In the middle of dinner?"

Mike: "I'm working on a physics project with Amber Alley. She's going to the library tonight—"

Mom: "I didn't think kids went to the library anymore. They just go online."

Mike: "Mr. Clayton is very old-fashioned. He wants us to look stuff up in books."

Mom: "Libraries aren't open at this hour."

Mike: "Mr. Clayton arranged for a branch to stay open late."

Already Mike's better at lying. He enjoys how he can invent a kind of parallel universe—physics projects that don't exist, old-fashioned teachers, libraries that stay open late. "So I need to catch Amber before she leaves the house."

Mom (slowly): "Amber Alley. Wasn't she the one you did that butterfly thing with?"

Mike (surprised): "Yeah—you remember that?" He's thinking it's kind of nice that she did.

Don't be fooled. She's not on your side. Look what she's making you eat. Now call Amber.

Mike goes to his room and calls Amber.

Amber answers on the first ring, almost as if she was waiting for the call.

Amber: "Hi, Mike."

Mike: "My mom just cooked this thing with meat and potatoes and butter. She's just sitting there, waiting for me to eat it."

Amber: "Did you eat it yet?"

Mike: "One bite."

Amber: "Okay, that's not so bad. Just eat five bites in total. Smush the food around on your plate. Keep count, though, and don't go over."

Mike: "Why five?"

Amber: "My friend Anna told me it's a good number—it makes you look like you're eating more than you actually are."

Five. The number of fingers on your hand. It's your own version of the right-hand rule.

Amber: "But you need to do more. Go to Food-A-Rama after school, buy some extra food to cook and throw out."

Mike: "What? Why?"

Amber: "To make it look like you're eating during the day. That way, if they're watching you, you can get away with eating less at night."

Mike thinks of the homeless guy, who needs to beg to eat, and the fact that Amber's telling Mike to buy food and purposely throw it away.

Mike: "Isn't that a waste?"

Amber: "It's the price to pay for privacy."

Exactly.

Amber: "Buy heavy, filling foods that are easy to make. Nothing diet or low fat. Macaroni and cheese, casseroles, creamy soups, Hungry-Man dinners. After school prepare the food and even put a plate in the sink with food scraped off. Be sure to take a fork with some food on it and smooth your lips over it, giving it that 'after eating' look. This girl I know, she forgot the fork, and her mom caught her."

Mike thinks it's a good thing he made money this summer, even if he's going to spend it on food he won't eat.

Amber: "At dinner, between the five bites, put food in a napkin on your lap. Throw that in the garbage when you're done. If your mom starts looking in the garbage—"

Mike: "That's gross. She wouldn't do that."

Amber: "Don't be so sure. Anyway, you can put food in a Ziploc freezer bag, the kind with the zipper, and throw the food away once you get outside. Too bad you don't have a dog. I know this girl—her dog would eat all her food for her. Except her dad got suspicious when he saw the dog sitting there every night at dinner, right at her feet. What about your dad? Is he giving you a hard time, too?"

Mike hasn't even told Tamio.

It's none of Tamio's business.

He thinks, Why should I tell Amber?

Why shouldn't you? Amber is a real friend.

Mike (with a sigh): "My dad moved out. He got a girlfriend. She's practically young enough to——"

Amber: "You're so lucky! One less pair of eyes on you at home."

Mike pushes the shepherd's pie around on his plate and puts piles along the edges. It looks like a clock face. He eats bites at two, six, eight, and ten o'clock (skipping the bites at twelve and four because of the one he ate before he called Amber). In between, he puts food in a napkin on his lap.

Mike: "That was really good."

Mom (disappointed): "You used to have more helpings. Except for the peas, of course, which you picked out one by one——"

Mike: "I'll have more later. I like it cold." More lies. Easy as pie, so to speak.

His mom does the dishes and laundry that night for the first time in forever, and even cleans up after Mighty Joe Young too. Mike wonders why she's doing better, then goes to his room and does fifty crunches and thirty push-ups. He stands before the mirror. He looks at himself closely, studying every inch, every pore. He used to think he was crazy for doing this, but now he wonders, If I am crazy, do I even care?

He doesn't.

Later that night Mike's stomach feels like a cliff that drops off into empty space. He is too hungry. He goes to the kitchen and opens the freezer. He sees rocky road ice cream. He grabs a spoon and digs out a huge scoop——

If you eat that, you'll get sick.

He thinks, Ice cream can't make me sick. He takes a bite. It's cool and smooth on his tongue, the way it slides down his throat . . . and then he feels it. Dizziness, cramping. He looks at the label. One-quarter cup has 17 grams of fat and 260 calories! He puts the rest of the spoonful into the sink and turns on the hot water full blast. He watches the ice cream melt down into bubbles.

Get rid of the rest of it.

He spoons the entire pint into the sink. He has to pick out the nuts from the drain. It takes a while for all the bubbles to dissolve.

In the refrigerator he sees some low-fat rice pudding he picked up with Amber. Rice pudding has always been a favorite of Mike's. He thinks about a place in Belle Heights called Luncheonette; it offers a dozen flavors of rice pudding; Mike and his parents used to order three different kinds and share—

Just finish up here and get some sleep.

Mike eats a cup of rice pudding and goes to bed.

The next day at lunch he tells Amber, "Thanks for the advice. It's really helping me."

Amber grins. Mike thinks her teeth look kind of filmy, that she should brush better. He's much too critical. Her teeth look fine.

Amber: "I wouldn't do this for some girl, you know."

Mike: "What?"

Amber: "You're not some girl who just wants to be skinnier than me."

Mike: "Um . . . yeah. So I got through dinner, but I got incredibly hungry later so I had one of those cups of rice pudding."

Amber: "Only half a cup, right?"

Mike: "No. The whole thing."

Amber: "You don't mean an entire cup, do you?"

Mike: "Yeah, that's what I just said."

Amber (quietly, like a doctor delivering bad news): "You had four grams of fat and four hundred and forty calories."

Mike: "No way. I read the label, like you told me. One serving has two grams of fat and two hundred and twenty calories."

Amber: "But each cup is two servings."

Mike: "What? Those cups are so small."

Amber: "Even so."

Mike: "No way." But this is the kind of thing Amber knows. Mike feels awful.

Amber (sadly): "I told you to be careful. When you get really hungry, try FireBalls."

When Mike gets home, his mom is cooking dinner again. Meat loaf this time. He cuts back to four bites, to make up for the rice pudding.

Mike goes to the mirror. He feels better. He can see muscle and taut skin. He thinks about his body, the structure of it, how each part is splendidly connected to the next; it is a work of art, like sculpture; it possesses power and energy.

Your mind is soaring!

CHAPTER 15

IT'S THE HEIGHT OF AUTUMN AND MIKE IS HAPPY.

He's never felt like this before, not in such a pure, undiluted form. Bursts of absolute joy fill his chest. He sees his boring old neighborhood in a whole new way. The slanting light makes everything pop as if it exists in more than three dimensions, a kind of super diorama—front lawn, sidewalk, street, bus, trees, sky, universe, beyond-the-universe. Tamio once told him that when he first put contacts in, he could see the veins in leaves. Mike thinks this is way better than that. When he looks at trees, he can see their life force, how mighty and solid they are. Colors are incredible. The awning over a fruit stand isn't simply green, it is glowing-green, green-on-fire. After a run in the park, Mike stops and stares at some flowers. The bright yellows and oranges look otherworldly, as if he has just landed in some distant galaxy and this is the plant life. He wonders, What are those flowers?

An old lady stands next to Mike. She has short white curly hair and so does the poodle she has with her.

Old Lady: "Don't you just love chrysanthemums?"

The universe is truly on your wavelength these days. You were wondering what the flowers were, and now somebody has told you.

Mike feels like he's living in an alternate reality, a reality he never knew he wanted. Here, things go right; here, everything feels new and mind-expanding; here, everything is in its right place.

Old Lady: "You know, you should rest, young man; you're bright red."

Mike gets mad. What is she, he thinks, my mother? He leaves without a word. He goes back to running even though he has finished his run. Amber told him he'd be able to run faster without all that dead weight holding him back. He runs until he can't run anymore.

But always finish the lap.

He runs. His legs cramp and there's a sharp pain in his chest. He can barely breathe.

Run past your endurance. That's how you build up strength.

He runs some more.

When Mike gets home, his phone is ringing.

Mike: "Hello?"

No answer. He sees a number he doesn't recognize on the caller ID.

Mike (louder): "Hello?" He finds it hard to catch his breath. He's practically gasping into the phone.

There's a low voice on the other end: "Hello."

Mike: "My mom's not home." He doesn't know if she's home

or not. "Do you want to leave a message?" Though he has no intention of writing anything down.

On the other end: "A message? No. It's Val."

Mike actually has to sit down.

Valerie: "I hope it's okay that I'm calling you."

It isn't. What could she possibly have to say?

Valerie: "I've been talking to Tamio. He says you're, I don't know, having a hard time or something. We both thought maybe you'd talk to me. You were so nice to me when I first came to school. So I thought I'd return the favor."

Mike can't get this straight. First Valerie's friendly. Then she's freaked out by him. Then she ignores him. Now she's friendly again. And she and Tamio have been talking about him behind his back?

She's far too unstable to be trustworthy. She could turn on you at any moment.

Valerie: "Are you there?"

Mike: "Where else would I be?"

Valerie: "Um . . . what?"

She heard you, all right.

Mike: "So you called me. You returned the favor—happy now?"

Valerie (big sigh): "Just forget it."

Mike: "Fine."

Valerie hangs up. The phone rings again. Another unknown number, though vaguely familiar—because it's the same one as a moment ago? Is it Valerie with Tamio beside her, both of them cracking up?

Mike (answering the phone): "What?"

On the other end: "My man."

It's Mike's dad. They haven't talked in weeks. It feels to Mike like a hundred years.

That's because time is passing more slowly for you. You're living your life more fully, absorbing every moment.

Dad (tapping the phone): "Hello?" The clicks are really annoying.

Mike: "I'm here."

Dad: "I'm glad I finally reached you. I called your cell and always got voice mail. I tried the house and always got the machine."

Mike wishes he'd let the machine get it this time, too.

Dad: "How are you?"

Mike: "Fine."

Dad: "How's your mother?"

What does he care?

Mike: "Fine."

Dad: "There have been some . . . changes."

Mike doesn't care about his dad and his changes. Why should he?

Dad: "We—well, there's no 'we' anymore. Laura and I split up."

Is he kidding? Mike tries to remember how long they were even together.

Dad: "She had this ex-boyfriend. He was out of town when we met. Anyway, he came back and, well, he's back." He's waiting for Mike to say something. But Mike has nothing to say. "It, uh . . . it wasn't easy for me. This thing with Laura—well, for one thing,

I had to find a place to live. I floated around awhile, finally found an apartment on Belle Boulevard near the expressway. Mike, it's good to talk to you."

This could go on forever. Hang up.

Mike: "Dad, I've got a lot of homework."

Dad: "Okay, I'll let you go. Let's have dinner soon—I'm close to some good Chinese restaurants."

Mike: "Sorry, I have too much work."

Mike unplugs the phone.

CHAPTER 16

IT'S TOO BAD MIKE CAN'T UNPLUG THE REST OF THE world.

Mom (at dinner): "Why are you wearing a sweatshirt? It's hot in here."

But the house is so cold, Mike thinks maybe the pipes burst. That happened one winter and they lit the oven to keep warm.

Mom: "You've even got your hood up."

Mike: "I'm fine."

Mom: "You look tired. Under your eyes, you look . . . bruised."

Mike: "I said I'm fine."

It's none of her business, if he's cold or not, how much sleep he gets or doesn't get. He does homework and studies at night, and works even better without Tamio around as a distraction. Three-page paper on insomnia in *Macbeth*? No problem—and unexpectedly appropriate. Test on free-body diagrams in physics? Easy A. Mike's grades have never been better. She's not complaining about that.

Mom: "Your father told me he spoke to you. He wanted to tell you himself, that he broke up with that woman."

Mike: "More like she broke up with him."

Mom (clearing her throat): "Maybe you're wondering where I've been these days. I'm making and keeping appointments. Isn't that good?"

Mike stares down at his chicken potpie. He takes his fourth bite. One more bite before he can go back to his room. Too bad it's a potpie—he can't make a clock face out of it. The bites in his napkin are burning his leg, but at least it feels warm.

Mom: "I'm seeing a therapist. Her name is Nora." Pause. "Are you listening?"

Mike: "You're working. You see a therapist. Nora."

Mom: "You sound so angry."

Mike: "I'm not angry!" Not about that, anyway. He's trying to keep count. He wonders, did I just eat my fifth bite, or put it in the napkin?

Don't let her ruin your concentration.

Mom: "Does it bother you, that I'm seeing a therapist?"

Mike: "Half the kids at school are in therapy."

Mom: "Do you want to know why I'm doing all this? Trying to pull myself together?" She's actually waiting for an answer.

Mike: "I give up."

Mom: "To help you."

Mike: "What! Why?"

Mom: "Because I can tell you're unhappy. You don't sound like yourself. You don't act like yourself. You need help, Mike."

Unbelievable. You've never been happier. This may be the first time in your life you don't need help. And where was she when you did?

Mom: "I wonder if you should be in therapy too."

Mike: "I'm doing great."

Mom: "You don't eat."

Mike: "I eat. You don't know what you're talking about." He realizes he forgot to cook this afternoon and throw food out. That must be what this is about. He thinks fast. "Today was Tamio's mom's birthday. I was over there for a party. There was pizza and cake." He gets a sudden ache, remembering Tamio's house, the sunny dining room, pictures of flowers, Tamio's mom, always so friendly. . . . He shoves a huge bite into his mouth.

That one counts as a double. You'll have to run extra laps tomorrow.

Mom: "How much do you weigh?"

Mike: "I don't know." He never gets on the scale. Numbers aren't important.

Mom: "You went to the doctor last spring. I'm going to look up your health record. Then I want to see what you weigh now." She pushes her chair back.

Mike doesn't want to get on the scale. She has no right.

Call Amber.

Again Amber answers on the first ring.

Mike: "My mom's making me get on the scale. What should I do?"

Amber: "Are you wearing clothes with pockets?"

*   *   *

Mike gets on the scale.

Mom (bending down to read the number): "It looks like you weigh—"

Mike: "I don't care."

Mom: "Well. You lost fifteen pounds. I thought you lost more." She doesn't sound too pleased.

Mike lets out a breath of relief. Those brass paperweights his dad left behind weigh a ton. They fit right into his pants pockets, front and back, and in his sweatshirt pockets too. The metal hunting dog is hidden in his fist.

Good dog.

CHAPTER 17

ERIC, FROM THE BASEBALL TEAM, SEES MIKE IN THE hall and invites him over to watch the World Series. Mike doesn't even know who's in it this year.

Mike: "No, thanks. How's your . . . uh . . ." Eric is the kid who broke something and is out for the season.

Eric: "Growth plate."

Mike: "Right." He has no idea what a growth plate is. Does this mean Eric will stop growing? But Eric towers over him. He's tall enough. Mike wishes he were taller.

Eric: "It's healing."

Mike: "What is?"

Eric: "My growth plate." He laughs a big laugh. "You're kind of out of it."

That's rather insulting.

Mike: "I don't think I'm going to play this year, either."

I couldn't be prouder. Mike's getting his priorities straight.

Eric: "Why not?"

Mike (with a shrug): "Just doing my own thing. Running, working out."

Eric: "But you're so good."

So what? You're good at something that doesn't mean anything.

Eric: "You always saved my ass out there, catching those long flies. You tell the coach about this?"

Mike: "Not yet."

Eric: "He won't be happy."

But you'll be happy. That's the important thing.

Eric: "Why are you so fidgety? It's like you can't stand still."

Start wearing headphones in the hall. That way people will leave you alone.

At lunch, Mike sees Amber and she's got on layers and layers of clothes. It reminds him of that homeless man. Mike pushes the image away.

Amber: "My mom's such a bitch. I made the mistake of telling her I want to be a nutritionist. She laughed—she actually laughed!"

Mike: "But you'd be a great nutritionist. You know everything about food."

Amber: "I do, right?" She tears open a pack of saltines. "Get this." She spits cracker dust when she talks. "My mom eats at Burger King. She says it's because of her job but I don't believe it. I think she actually likes Whoppers."

Mike: "Your mom works at Burger King?"

Amber runs her fingers through her hair. Several strands come loose and float to the floor like bits of cobweb.

Amber: "If I tell you, you won't tell anyone?"

Mike: "Who am I gonna tell?"

Amber: "Tamio?"

Mike: "I told you. We're not friends."

Amber: "Well, all right." She whispers something Mike can't understand.

Mike: "She's a cool hunger?"

Amber (annoyed): "A cool hunter. She's hired by advertising companies to observe teenagers and see what they find cool. Isn't that the dumbest thing you ever heard? She goes to Burger King to see the clothes kids are wearing, the shoes they have on, the phones they're using." Amber has chicken soup today. She spoons out the noodles and puts them on her tray. "I hate her."

Mike nods.

Amber: "She hates all the friends I ever had."

Mike: "Anna?"

Amber: "Oh, she hates Anna more than anyone."

Mike: "What about your boyfriend?"

Amber: "We can't even talk about it. It makes her crazy. She hates everything about me. She hates what I wear. She wants me to look like Melissa Sacks, with her tight little skirts and thigh-high boots. Melissa is the daughter my mom had in mind when she thought about having one."

This is heartbreaking. Amber's mom should be so proud of

her. Amber, who is her own person, who doesn't want to look like everybody else. But Mike doesn't really like the way Amber's clothes hang on her, like she's got on a pile of laundry.

Mike: "I don't know . . . maybe your mom could get you some new clothes."

Amber: "It's never about me! It's about her. When she talks to me, I count the number of times she says 'I.' Then she gets mad and says I'm not listening. Even then it's all about her. 'I can tell,' she says. 'I always know.' See what I mean?"

Mike (nodding): "My dad can be like that—"

Amber: "Anyway, why should I listen to her? I could care less what she has to say." She rips open another pack of saltines. "I was really close to my aunt Claire. She died suddenly from an aneurism. You know what that is? It's when an artery fills with blood and bursts. My mom kept telling me to get over it. 'Look at me,' she said, 'I'm moving on.' God, I'm such a pig. My mom makes me crazy."

Mike: "Hey, are you crying?"

Amber: "No! I just hate her so much."

Mike thinks she sure looks like she's crying.

Mike: "What about your dad?"

Amber: "He's worse than useless. He thinks what my mom tells him to think."

Mike: "Well, it's good you have friends."

Amber: "Friends? When I was in the hospital last summer, for four whole weeks, no one came to see me. No one!"

Mike: "Why were you in the hospital?"

Amber: "What do you care?"

Mike: "Four weeks—that's a long time. What happened?"

Amber: "It did so happen. Are you accusing me of lying?"

She wasn't hearing Mike right. There's that lazy lip, rearing its ugly head, so to speak.

Mike: "I asked you what happened. If you don't understand me, just say so."

Amber: "I understand you better than you think!"

Mike: "Huh?"

Amber: "Drop dead." She stands. She nearly falls over.

Mike grabs her by the arm.

Mike: "You okay?"

Amber: "Let go of me!" She leaves the cafeteria.

Amber is emotional and she feels things deeply. All the most interesting people are like that.

Mike cleans up after her: the saltine wrappers, the crumbs, the soggy noodles.

Tamio's in the hall—the last person Mike wants to see.

Tamio: "Look at this." Tamio has his cell phone open. There's a picture. It's a guy, hunched over, in a jacket that's too big for him. He looks old and wasted. Homeless or something.

Mike: "Um, okay. What is this?"

Tamio: "That's you."

Mike: "No way."

Tamio: "Look again if you don't believe me."

Mike: "I don't need to look. I already know it's not me."

Tamio: "See, it's your black North Face jacket—"

Mike: "Everyone has a jacket like that."

Tamio: "Maybe, but nobody else is wearing theirs yet." He starts waving at the air. "What's that smell?"

Mike: "FireBalls."

Tamio: "What'd you say?"

Mike is stunned. Tamio always understood him, or so Mike thought.

Tamio: "I only took your picture so you could see for yourself. You look terrible. Don't you ever look in a mirror?"

Ha. If Tamio only knew how many hours Mike spends in front of a mirror. Anyway, Mike only looks in his mirror at home, which tells him all he needs to know. He doesn't trust other mirrors.

Mike: "I look fine. What's your problem?"

Tamio: "What's my problem? What's wrong with you?"

Tamio's jealous. You're getting yourself together, without his help.

Mike: "You wish you were me, asshole."

Tamio: "What?"

But Mike can tell—Tamio heard him that time, all right.

After school Mike wants to run, but it's raining.

You can run in the rain.

Mike runs. The rain is exquisite, the way it's highlighted against the streetlights, a spray of glistening drops against silver-white light.

See what you would've missed if you stayed home?

Mike works out in his room. Seventy-five crunches, fifty push-ups. When he breathes in, he can feel his ribs.

Strong body, strong mind. Infinitely strong.

Amber calls. Mike thinks maybe she's still mad, but she says, "I'm so happy! I lost four pounds. I hated being in the hundreds."

Her voice drops to a whisper:

"I love that there is less of me."

CHAPTER 18

IT'S ALMOST HALLOWEEN, TRICK-OR-TREAT TIME. Kids at school are talking parties and costumes. Not Mike. He has far more important ways to spend his time. Speaking of trick-or-treat, Mike's mom is full of surprises, and none of them good.

Mom: "I made an appointment for you this Friday. You're going to my doctor."

Mike: "What for?"

Mom: "You need to see a specialist."

Mike: "Why?"

Mom: "You're too thin and you know it."

Mike: "I'm not. I got on the scale—"

Mom: "I don't care. You're always dressed like it's snowing in here while it's hot as hell in the house."

Mike yanks off his jacket and sweatshirt. Unfortunately his shirt slides up too.

Mom (breathes in): "Oh, my God."

Mike: "What?"

Mom: "Your chest . . . it's caving in on itself."

Mike knows she's seeing it wrong. When he looks in the mirror, he sees results from his hard work.

She'll never understand the way you're fine-tuning your body. She can't appreciate it.

Mom: "You're going to the doctor and that's final."

Of course Mike can't stuff his dad's paperweights into a paper gown at a doctor's office. He feels a stab of panic.

Call Amber.

Amber's right there, as always.

Amber: "Drink lots of water before you go, and I mean lots. In the waiting room, drink even more. You can put on a good five pounds that way. Temporarily, of course."

Mike: "What if this doctor can, you know, tell? Take one look at me and figure it out?"

Amber: "Doctors are idiots. They're so easy to manipulate. Just tell them what they want to hear."

Mike: "And what's that?"

Amber: "They practically tell you what to say. It's like being in a school play and they're feeding you your next lines."

At the doctor's office, Mike's mom paces in the waiting room.

Mom: "My doctor's not here. She has a family emergency. You have to see someone else."

Mike drinks another paper cup of water. It's shaped like a cone with a sharp needle point at the bottom.

Mike: "It's fine."

Mom: "It's not. I don't have a good feeling about it. I don't know this doctor."

It could be Dr. Seuss, for all Mike cares. He really has to go to the bathroom. He drank a gallon of water at home and he's gulping down another gallon here.

Mike and his mom are called into the doctor's office. The desk is covered with piles of papers. Mike's mom stiffens at the sight of it.

Doctor: "I'm Dr. Steiner." He's over six feet tall with deeply lined skin and black hair that curls over his forehead. He probably dyes his hair. "Hello, Michael, nice to meet you."

That's good. Michael is an adult, mature name. Mike sounds too curt and abrupt, or like the object you talk into so your voice can be heard.

But Mike's mom has to put in her two cents: "Nobody calls him that. It's Mike."

Mike: "It's okay. Nice to meet you, too."

Doctor: "Do you mind, Mrs. Welles, if Michael and I speak privately?"

She minds, all right, but she leaves the room. She even closes the door behind her.

Doctor: "Your mother's very concerned about you, Michael. Is there anything you wish to tell me?"

Tell him what's going on, how your mother can't cope.

Mike: "My parents just split up. It's really hard on my mom. She can't leave the house. I mean, she left today, but not usually. She sleeps a lot during the day. She takes baths that last for hours."

Doctor: "I see."

Mike gets a stab of guilt. I try to tell him to ignore it, but he says, "Lately she's better. She goes to a therapist. She's working again."

Doctor: "Mm."

No matter—the damage is done. The doctor thinks Mike's mom is unhinged.

Doctor: "Now, Michael, I want to ask you a few questions. Just between us; your mother will not be privy to the answers. Do you take drugs?"

Amber was right. The doctor is practically shaking his head as he asks this.

Mike: "No."

Doctor: "Are you sexually active?"

Mike: "No."

Doctor: "No trouble at school? No failing grades?"

Mike: "I'm getting all As."

Doctor: "Excellent. You're not dieting, are you, Michael?"

Mike: "No."

Doctor (grinning): "You seem fine so far. Let's check you out, shall we?"

Dr. Steiner leads Mike to a cold room with a doctor's scale and a metal table covered with crinkly white paper. The doctor tells Mike to put on a paper gown and discreetly waits outside the door. Mike badly needs the bathroom. Dr. Steiner comes in and tells Mike to stand on the scale.

Don't worry about the number. What matters is how you look, not what you weigh.

Doctor: "According to your record, you've lost about thirty pounds since the spring."

Ha, with all that water, make it closer to thirty-five.

Doctor (raising the bar that measures height): "You're five nine and a half."

Mike: "I didn't grow at all in six months?"

Doctor: "I'm sorry—what?"

Don't worry about it. Growth comes in stages.

Mike: "Never mind."

The doctor moves on to Mike's blood pressure. It's taking all of Mike's concentration not to pee.

Doctor: "Well, Michael, your weight's a little low for your height, and your blood pressure's a little low too. Do you exercise? That might explain it."

Mike: "I run."

Doctor: "Good for you! So do I, when the knees don't bother me. You've got to watch the knees, especially when you're an old fart like me. Are you cold? I try to keep it warm in here."

Mike (teeth chattering): "I'm fine."

Doctor: "Look at that, your finger's bleeding."

Mike looks down. The cut, from the day he bought the mirror. He doesn't know how it opened up again. Did the paper cup stab him?

Mike: "Is it okay if I go to the bathroom?"

Doctor: "Go right ahead."

After Mike goes to the bathroom and gets his clothes back on, he returns to Dr. Steiner's office. His mom is there.

Mom: "Don't you think he's too thin?"

Doctor (slowly, like he's talking to a child): "I know what you're thinking, Mrs. Welles. What all the girls are getting—anorexia nervosa." He says it like it's Italian food. "Michael's just a skinny teenager, like we all were, once upon a time." He laughs.

Mom: "He barely eats. He skips breakfast. Who knows what he has for lunch? At dinner I see him pushing his food around—"

Mike: "I eat after school. That's when I get hungry. I make some mac and cheese—"

Mom: "But you don't eat it! You throw it all away!"

Amber was right. His mom goes through the garbage. Dr. Steiner gives Mike a look of sympathy, for his crazy mom. Dr. Steiner stands. He casts a shadow over Mike and his mom.

Doctor: "Mrs. Welles, Michael's in excellent shape." Unlike you, he seems to imply. The doctor is smiling. Mike is smiling. I am smiling, in my way.

Mike's mom is not.

CHAPTER 19

ACCORDING TO THE WEATHER REPORTS, IT'S UNSEASON-ably warm for November. Then why does it feel to Mike like Belle Heights is ushering in a new ice age? At any moment he expects to see icebergs floating down the expressway. But, freezing weather aside, life is perfect. Mike and I are in sync, partners in the project that is Mike. He works out until his body sings—that's how it feels, this pain that is also not-pain, because its intensity is so satisfying. He looks in the mirror and admires the tightness of his skin, the clean lines of his body. He is focused. If his mind ever drifts to unpleasant topics, I put him back on track:

Strong body, strong mind. Everything in its right place.

Mike takes Amber's advice and starts putting the food he's not eating in Ziploc bags. He stashes them all over the house—behind shelves, under his bed, in the corners of closets. But sometimes he forgets to take them outside, and one night his mom says, "It smells like something died in here."

Mike tries to remember all his hiding places, but it's difficult. He has so much on his mind.

Mom: "I think it's a mouse." She sounds frightened. "I always thought, because of Mighty Joe Young, mice would stay away. Could you look around? Just the thought of finding a dead mouse . . ." She shivers.

Mike finds bags of rotting food hidden everywhere. The worst offender is in the coat closet, near the front door—a moldy greenish-brownish mush of something in the pocket of a jacket belonging to his dad.

Mom: "Did you find anything?"

Mike: "A dead mouse in the coat closet. In the corner, all curled up."

Mom: "Oh! Poor thing."

When Mike tells Amber about it, she laughs and laughs. She finds it hilarious that his mom feels sorry for a mouse that never existed.

Now Tamio's waiting for Mike outside homeroom. Before Mike can brush past him, Tamio says, "Amber's in the hospital."

Mike: "No way. I just talked to her."

Tamio: "When was that?"

Mike has to think. He wonders why it's so hard to concentrate sometimes.

Because your mind is on important things.

Mike tries to remember his most recent conversation with Amber. It feels like they talk all the time, but he realizes they haven't actually spoken since lunch on Friday. Today is Monday. The weekend—running, working out, looking in the mirror—flew by.

Tamio: "She had a heart attack."

Mike: "You're crazy. She's too young."

Tamio: "Well, she screws up her body. She makes herself throw up."

Mike: "Where'd you hear that?"

Tamio: "Why do you think she's always trying to cover it up with those candies? Like the ones I smell on you."

That is not why Amber likes FireBalls. But never mind. Mike is so upset, his hands start shaking.

Calm down. Tamio doesn't even know Amber, remember?

Mike (taking a deep breath): "You don't know anything about Amber."

Tamio: "I figured you knew. I thought maybe you were trying to help her out."

Mike: "She doesn't need help. She's happy. She's the happiest person I know." Mike remembers how Amber almost fell down in the cafeteria. "She probably just broke her ankle."

Tamio: "Dude. It's not her ankle."

The bell rings.

All day everyone is talking about Amber.

Melissa Sacks (stopping Mike in the hall): "Have you seen her in the hospital? Is she okay? A heart attack! That's, like, such a huge thing. Is there anything I can do?"

Mike remembers Melissa pretending to stick her finger down her throat at the sight of Amber. She can go to hell, that's what she can do.

Finally Mike makes it to the last class of the day. He's exhausted. Mr. Clayton is talking about a new star system that's just been discovered. Apparently Mr. Clayton is the only one excited about it.

Mr. Clayton: "Imagine—a triple-sun system! The main sun is bright yellow. There's also a large orange sun and a small red one. It's one of the oddest places in our galaxy."

When class ends and kids pile out, Mr. Clayton looks right at Mike.

Mr. Clayton: "Can I talk to you for a sec?"

Mike wants to go home, call Amber, run, work out. He wishes he were anywhere else, even in that triple-sun system, which at least sounds warm.

As Mike approaches Mr. Clayton's desk, Mr. Clayton says, "Your finger's bleeding."

Mike looks down. It's covered in blood. He wonders why he never feels it. Why hasn't it healed yet?

Some things take time.

Mike (all innocence): "Is that what you wanted to tell me, about my finger?"

Mr. Clayton: "I'm concerned about you, Mike. Several times you seemed to lose your balance. I thought you might pass out."

It's unfortunate that Mr. Clayton noticed that. The last class of the day is always the hardest to get through because Mike is so eager to leave and get on with his life. Sometimes he stands up too fast and he's short of breath and the room goes suddenly dark. But it only lasts a moment.

It gets hot in here and that makes you dizzy.

Mike: "Yeah, well, it gets hot in here and I get a little dizzy."

Mr. Clayton: "Maybe you should take your jacket off, then."

Mike (with a shrug): "I guess I forget I have it on."

Mr. Clayton: "You've lost weight."

You were sick. You had the flu.

Mike: "I had the flu."

Mr. Clayton: "You didn't miss school."

Mike: "Yeah, I had it over the weekend. It was a weekend-only kind of thing."

Mr. Clayton: "My nephew looked a lot like you, not long ago. It turns out he was really sick."

Mike: "I just got a checkup from a doctor. He said I was fine."

Mr. Clayton: "My nephew had five checkups, and five doctors told him he was fine. But he was really sick."

Does Mr. Clayton have more medical expertise than five doctors?

Mr. Clayton: "Now he's on the road to recovery."

Mike: "Who?"

Mr. Clayton (carefully): "My nephew."

This is so tedious.

Mike: "The road to recovery. That's good."

Mr. Clayton: "It's a long road."

Mike: "Well, at least he's on it."

Mr. Clayton: "My nephew was on the wrestling team. His coach wanted him to be a certain weight. He stopped eating, just—stopped. He exercised like crazy. He ran for hours. He could do hundreds of sit-ups."

Don't be jealous. You'll get there.

Mr. Clayton: "His parents told him he couldn't run. He snuck out in the middle of the night, and his body just gave out. He collapsed, hit his head, needed seventeen stitches."

His parents shouldn't have told him he couldn't run. That's how accidents happen.

Mr. Clayton: "He almost died. He could've bled to death."

Mike: "Well, at least he didn't." Mike turns to leave. "See you tomorrow."

Mr. Clayton: "You take care of yourself, now."

It sounds like a threat.

CHAPTER 20

MIKE CAN'T GET THROUGH TO AMBER ON HER CELL— it goes straight to voice mail. He looks up her number and calls her house.

Woman: "Hello?"

Mike: "Hi, this is Mike Welles."

Woman: "Amber said you might call." Of course it's Amber's mom, but she doesn't identify herself. Her tone is so flat, she sounds like a computer. I take an instant dislike to her, but Mike reserves judgment.

Mike: "Is Amber all right?"

Amber's mom: [nothing]

Mike: "Hello?"

Amber's mom: "I can't go into it right now. You can't call her directly. You can visit if you want. Let me give you her information, the hospital and visiting hours."

Mike writes it all down.

Mike: "I know that hospital. My grandmother died there."

Oops.

Mike: "Different floor."

Amber's mom: "Is that all?"

Mike: "I heard something happened with her heart?"

Amber's mom: "Like I said, I can't go into it right now. I've got a lot on my plate."

Mike thinks that's an odd way to put it, considering.

Later Mike is so hungry he can't sleep. Even FireBalls don't help. He feels like there's an animal in his stomach, clawing him with huge talons, taking him apart from the inside. He wishes he could call Amber. How did Amber know Mike would need to call her in the middle of the night? She's so intuitive, almost clairvoyant.

Mike goes to the kitchen. Mighty Joe Young is digging into his Feline Fine.

Mike: "Don't throw up."

Mighty Joe Young looks up at him with large copper eyes. Mike wonders if the cat is thinking about what he just said. Mike tries to remember what Amber told him she eats when she can't sleep.

Carrots dipped in mustard.

Mike takes a carrot out of the refrigerator. It's pale and limp. He opens up some horseradish mustard. Amber recommended it—she likes strong mustards. Mike sticks in the carrot, takes a bite.

Mike: "Gahhh!" It makes his eyes water. He thinks if he takes another bite, he'll throw up, along with Mighty Joe Young.

Amber also drinks lemon juice in water. Mike pours out a glass of water and splashes in some lemon juice. He takes a sip and finds it disgusting. He wonders if Amber has any taste buds left or if all those FireBalls killed them off.

There's a loaf of bread. Before I can say anything, Mike grabs the loaf and takes it back to his room like a thief. He pulls out a slice, stuffs it into his mouth.

Don't eat that, don't eat that, don't eat that.

He removes it from his mouth. It's a soggy ball of bread. He puts it on the windowsill and stares at it. Then he shoves it back into his mouth.

Don't eat that, don't eat that, don't eat that.

He takes it out again, puts it back on the windowsill. It looks like a snowball. He takes out another slice and does the exact same thing. Why is he doing this? Soon he's got five snowballs on his windowsill.

And he remembers:

In Belle Heights Park, after a snowstorm. Mike throws a snowball at his dad. His dad fires one back—misses. Mike throws one at his mom and she lets out a shrieky laugh: "Ah, it hurts my teeth! I'll get you for that!" Her aim is perfect. Another snowstorm. Mike and his parents build a snowman in Belle Heights Park. The next day somebody puts a hat on it, a real old-fashioned hat from the 1940s. No question about it, Mike thinks, he's the classiest snowman in all of Belle Heights. Another snowstorm. Mike wears sneakers in the snow and his feet get really cold and wet. He is seven—a big boy—but his dad carries him home.

Mike keeps putting the snowballs back in his mouth, chewing them, spitting them out. Eventually they fall apart and he throws them away. The behavior is bizarre, but I'm pleased he doesn't actually eat them.

Mike doesn't know what else to do. He starts taking down all his baseball posters. That's fine—he should've done this long ago. They rip. He doesn't care. He wants totally empty walls, except for the mirror.

All you need to look at is you.

CHAPTER

21

THE HOSPITAL IS ON THE FAR SIDE OF BELLE Heights, and Mike takes the Q33 bus to get there. He rides the elevator up to Amber's floor. When he gets off, he sees a large room with a TV and some couches. It's dark except for flickers of light from the TV. Several girls are there. One girl is skinny. Scary-skinny, Mike thinks. She has a needle in her arm, attached to a pole with a bag of fluids. She sees Mike staring at her. Mike wonders if she's embarrassed by this. She yawns.

His sneakers squeak on the shiny floor. There are nurses every-where—at desks, walking around. A nurse tells Mike that Amber is in the Sun Room. He has to pass a series of closed doors before he gets to an open one with a hand-drawn picture of the sun on it. He sees Amber sitting on a couch. The room is empty except for her. She's got on a white T-shirt and jeans. Mike has never seen her arms before. He thinks she looks thin but nothing like the girl with the pole.

It's good, really good, to see Amber again.

Amber (smiling a sneaky smile): "So how do you like the E-D unit?"

Mike: "E-D?"

Amber: "I told you about my boyfriend, Eddie, remember? It's a joke. 'E-D' stands for 'eating disorder.'" She laughs.

Mike: "Eddie's not your boyfriend?"

Mike can be a little dense sometimes.

Amber: "No, Eddie's not my boyfriend!"

Mike wonders why Amber thinks it's funny that she lies to people about having a boyfriend.

She has a sense of humor.

Mike: "So when can you go home?"

Amber: "Well, it's my second time, so I have to stay longer. It's like a rule. Last time I had a bed near the window. This time my bed is near the door. Sit down, will you? You're making me nervous."

Mike sits on a padded chair that looks soft but it's like a rock.

Mike: "So this is the Sun Room."

Amber: "It's never sunny, by the way, but it's usually empty and it's good to have some alone time. I have a roommate. Her name is Deirdre. The staff calls her a frequent flier because she's been here three times already. I'm so jealous of her."

Mike: "Because she's a frequent flier?"

Amber: "No! Because she's so much skinnier than me."

Mike: "Is she in the TV room?"

Amber: "I think so. She's blond."

Mike didn't notice the color of her hair.

Amber: "Deirdre's so beautiful. Anyone can have inner beauty. Not everyone has real beauty. She's a size double zero."

Mike: "How is that even possible?"

Amber: "Deirdre used to do ballet. She was good, too. But she can't dance anymore. Whatever. She does a different kind of dance now. She dances between the raindrops in the rain."

Mike: "Dances between the—what?"

Amber: "It's an expression. Like, I want to stand in the sun and cast no shadow. Or move as lightly as a spider, not even disturbing a web."

Mike: "I never heard those expressions."

Amber: "Just because you never heard of something doesn't mean it isn't meaningful."

Mike takes a deep breath.

You could at least smile at her. Stop acting like you're at a funeral.

Amber: "So is everybody at school talking about me? Not that I care."

Mike: "They say you had a heart attack."

Amber: "See? That's wrong." She says something Mike can't understand, so she spells it out: "A-r-r-h-y-t-h-m-i-a. It's an uneven heartbeat. They say it can lead to a heart attack."

Mike (thinking it sounds bad): "Isn't that bad?"

Amber: "It's not even why I came to the hospital. Didn't my mom explain?"

Mike shakes his head.

Amber: "She's such a bitch! You know what she did? She took away my red bracelet. She found out what it meant. Red for anorexia. A-N-A for short."

Anna—the best friend. Who doesn't exist. Just like Eddie. Mike's getting freaked out by the fact that Amber doesn't have a best friend or a boyfriend. It's sad, he thinks.

It's not sad. Amber has something better than friends.

She doesn't have anyone, Mike thinks.

You are her friend.

Amber: "My wrist feels so naked. Can you get me another bracelet? You can only buy them online. You probably don't have your own credit card, so you'll have to use your mom's." She shivers. "It's cold in here."

Mike: "You want my jacket?"

Amber: "Thanks."

It's big and puffy on her.

Mike: "Amber, if you didn't come here for a heart rhythm—"

Amber: "Arrhythmia. Try to get it right."

Mike: "—then why are you here?"

Amber (with that sneaky smile again): "Remember, Friday night, there was a new moon?"

Mike: "No."

Amber: "Well, there was. The new moon is when you honor Anamadim. She's the goddess of anorexia."

Mike: "The goddess of—what?"

Amber: "I'm not surprised you never heard of her. I only just learned about her recently."

Mike knows something about gods and goddesses, mostly because they pop up in Harryhausen's movies, but, he thinks, a goddess of anorexia—?

There's a god or goddess for everything under the sun. Listen to Amber.

Amber: "I had to sneak out of the house and make a sacrifice to Anamadim."

Mike (not sure he wants to know): "What'd you sacrifice?"

Amber: "Food that tempts me. I took some saltines and crushed them in my front yard. Back in my room, I pledged to Anamadim: 'Fill me with the ecstasy of emptiness, empower me to endure the necessary deprivations, make light the vessel where I sojourn upon this earth.'"

Mike thinks, She's having a religious experience over saltines.

She cares about something, deeply.

Amber (with a laugh): "It's a bit much, I know, but it really helps me, okay? To reach my goals. Anyway, I had to write down the pledge and then sign it in blood. Wouldn't you know it—that's when my mom woke up. The problem was, when I cut my wrist, I used a really sharp steak knife—"

Mike (alarmed): "You cut your wrist?"

Amber: "I wasn't trying to kill myself! I just made a tiny cut, here." She shows him a spot on the side of her wrist, where she has a Band-Aid. "Anyway, it wouldn't stop bleeding. My mom flipped out. She thought I was a cutter. Like she knows anything. If I was a cutter, I'd wear a black-and-blue bracelet."

Mike: "They have bracelets for cutters?"

Amber: "And purple for bulimia, where you throw up after you eat. Which is disgusting. I only throw up when I absolutely have to."

Tamio was right, Mike thinks; Amber does throw up.

Who cares? He never applies himself to anything worthwhile.

Amber: "Anyway, my mom took me straight to the hospital." She shrugs. "The cut was no big deal. It didn't even need stitches. But that's when they told my mom I was severely emaciated. C'mon, do I look severely emaciated to you? Also they found the arrhythmia. And the fact that the mass of my heart had decreased. Weird, huh? I didn't know hearts could do that."

Mike: "Amber, are you scared?"

Amber: "No, I'm just mad because I'm stuck here for six weeks, maybe longer."

Mike notices a closed door in the corner of the room.

Mike: "What's that?"

Amber: "The bathroom. It's locked. All the bathrooms are locked. You have to ask permission to go. And they watch you, to make sure you're not throwing up. They even watch you in the shower. There's zero privacy here. Before they weigh you, they do a cavity search."

Mike: "A what?"

Amber: "Some people put rolls of quarters in their butts."

Mike wants to leave. He wonders what he's doing here in the first place. Do I even know this person? he thinks.

Of course you do.

I don't, not really, he thinks. Amber's always telling me all this stuff she does, but actually nothing about herself, if that makes any sense—

It doesn't.

Amber had an aunt who died, and they were close—

Why bring up something painful? You know what you need to know.

Mike stands. The chair sticks to him.

Mike: "I have to go."

Amber: "Okay. Will you come back?"

Mike doesn't want to.

You'll come back.

Mike: "Sure." He notices, for the first time, Amber's eyelashes. They're so sparse. He thinks those eyelashes, and his jacket, make her look like a little kid, lost and alone.

She's neither.

Amber takes off Mike's jacket and gives it back to him.

Amber: "Hey, will you tell that witch outside that it's freezing in here?"

Mike goes to the nearest nurse at a desk. Her head is bent over a magazine.

Mike: "Hi, I was just in the Sun Room with Amber Alley. She's wondering if you could turn up the heat?"

Nurse: "They're always cold. Anyway, I can't change the thermostat. It's controlled." She doesn't look up.

Mike passes the TV room again. He sees Deirdre. Is she blond? Hard to tell. She doesn't have much hair, and the intermittent light from the TV gives him only strobelike glimpses. Someone is sitting next to her.

Mike stops.

He can't move.

It's a boy, Mike thinks. He sees short hair, sideburns . . . an Adam's apple.

You're seeing it wrong. It's a girl who looks like a boy.

I can't move, Mike thinks. I've turned to stone, like in *Clash of the Titans*, when Perseus's men look at Medusa—

You are not stone. You are living and breathing.

It's like I'm stuck between frames in a movie.

You can move. Just put one foot in front of the other. It's only a trick of the light.

CHAPTER 22

OUTSIDE THE HOSPITAL, EVERY STEP IS A STRUGGLE. Mike moves painfully slowly, sometimes stopping just to stare at a—what? A squashed leaf, an ancient cocker spaniel trudging along, a crack in the sidewalk.

There's the Q33 bus. Get on the bus.

Mike has to be led by the hand like a child, so to speak. He stands the whole ride home even though there are plenty of seats. He stoops over and looks out the window at the darkening sky—it gets dark early now. He starts thinking about another one of Harryhausen's movies, *The 7th Voyage of Sinbad*. For once I don't think this is a bad idea. Maybe it'll calm him down. He remembers the part where Sinbad fights a skeleton. But it reminds him of that girl, Deirdre. He thinks, She's practically a skeleton; she could end up like the skeleton in that movie, a pile of broken bones.

Don't let some silly movie upset you. When you get home, go straight to your room, turn on some music, work out.

To my relief, this is exactly what he does—150 crunches, 100 push-ups.

You are becoming infinitely strong.

Mike is sure, now, that he saw a girl at the hospital, a girl who only looked like a boy. That kind of mistake happens all the time.

With some effort, Mike is himself again.

His mom knocks on his door. Quickly Mike puts on a T-shirt and then lets her in.

Mom: "Could you turn the music down, please? The walls are shaking."

Mike turns it down.

Mom: "Have you had dinner?"

Mike: "I ate in the hospital cafeteria."

Mom (clearly not believing him but asking anyway): "What'd you have?"

Mike: "Grilled cheese and fries." He's memorized what to say by now. He has whole menus in his head.

Mom: "You're having lunch with your father on Saturday."

Mike: "What? Why?"

Mom: "He's your father."

Mike: "So?"

Mom: "It's been a long time. He wants to see you."

No one's asking if you want to see him.

Mom: "He'll meet you at a Chinese restaurant. I wrote down the address."

Mike: "What's the name of it?"

Mom: "I don't think he told me—just that it's on the corner of Belle Terrace and Seventy-Fourth Lane."

Mike: "Mom, I need the name."

Mom: "Why?"

So Mike can look up the menu online and see what he can eat, that's why. He doesn't tell her that, though.

Mom: "Well, I don't think your father knows the name."

Mike: "That's so stupid."

Mom: "You'll find it. How hard can it be?"

Impossible, it turns out. Mike takes a bus to Belle Terrace and Seventy-Fourth Court, a block from Seventy-Fourth Lane. It's across from the expressway, and there aren't any restaurants, just fruit stands and depressing, down-on-their-luck stores. One place has mannequins with missing arms. Mike is feeling grumpy anyway because he fell asleep at dawn and woke up too late to go for a run.

A Chinese woman is staring at him. Mike knows what she's thinking: That boy didn't run today. He's so lazy.

Mike thinks, It's not my fault I have to meet my idiot father for lunch.

Mike (to the Chinese woman): "Stop staring at me!"

The Chinese woman looks at him blankly. Maybe she doesn't understand English. Or maybe she's only pretending not to.

Man's voice (behind Mike): "Mike, is that you?"

Mike turns around. It's his dad.

Dad: "I can't believe it."

Mike can't believe it, either. His dad has a potbelly. He's let himself get completely out of shape since the breakup.

Dad (barely above a whisper): "Your mother was right."

Mike: "Right about what?"

Dad: [nothing]

Mike: "So anyway, where's this restaurant?"

Dad (numbly, like he's in shock): "On the other side."

He means the other side of the expressway. What's his problem? He wanted to have lunch with Mike. Mike didn't want to have lunch with him.

The restaurant is large and noisy. Mike and his dad sit at a table in the corner, and a waitress hands them enormous menus.

Dad: "Let me order. I know what's good here."

Mike: "That's okay."

Dad: "You used to love sweet-and-sour chicken."

Well, things change.

Dad: "Can I get you the chicken?"

Mike: "No. I'll have steamed broccoli."

Dad: "That's hardly a meal."

Mike: "It's what I want."

Dad: "We can go to Luncheonette after. I know you love the rice pudding there."

Mike: "No, thanks." Mike's had enough rice pudding to last him the rest of his life.

They order. His dad gets the sweet-and-sour chicken.

Dad: "I hope you'll have some."

The food comes so fast, it's surprising they had time to cook it.

Mike takes the first of five bites of broccoli. That Chinese woman should see him now. His discipline, his self-control.

Dad: "I wanted to tell you. I've got a girlfriend."

Mike: "You're back with Laura?" Mike is fairly certain this is not what his dad meant, but he says it anyway.

Dad: "Terry is not like Laura."

Mike: "Is she younger?"

Dad: "Terry's older than I am. Not supermodel gorgeous, but attractive."

She's fat, in other words.

His dad says something about where Terry works. It sounds like she controls the city.

Mike: "What?"

Dad (more clearly): "Terry works for the city comptroller. That's the treasurer's office. They keep track of the money." Pause. "Your finger's bleeding."

Mike thinks, How many months has it been since I cut my finger?

Don't worry about it.

The clean white napkin in Mike's lap, the one holding most of the broccoli, now has several glistening drops on it, vivid and bright red. Mike thinks, Harryhausen was always careful to make his movie blood look real, but this blood looks fake.

Dad: "Try the chicken."

Mike: "No."

Dad: "Please. For me."

Mike looks at the chicken, orange and shiny. It looks fake, too.

Dad: "Just one bite?" He puts a piece on Mike's plate.

Mike lifts a fork to stab it. But he can't do it.

Dad: "What's wrong?"

Mike: "I can't."

Dad: "Can't—or won't?"

Mike is almost in tears. What's the matter with me? he thinks. It's like something else is controlling me. Is it my dad's new girlfriend, the controller of the city?

Dad: "Never mind. It's okay."

Mike thinks, It's not okay. I don't know what's going on. I'm not in control.

Yes, you are.

Why can't I eat the chicken?

Because you don't want to. It's disgusting.

I do want to. I mean, I'm willing to, but I can't.

You're in control.

But if I'm not, what is?

Mike overthinks, sometimes.

Again I have to work hard to calm Mike down, get him out of the restaurant and back on the bus, see to it that he goes for a run even before he goes home. Then he feels better. He's not even hungry as he runs.

You can run over hunger.

He stumbles a bit, bangs up his knee. No blood. He runs some more.

Back home, he looks in the mirror and sees something he's never seen before. There's a thin, fuzzy patch of hair on his shoulders.

A dusting of it on his stomach, too. It's soft, like a blanket. Nice, Mike thinks.

Don't see your dad anymore. It's too disruptive.

Mike agrees. He knows what's at stake here.

Don't see anyone anymore. Except for Amber.

Mike agrees to that, too. Besides, he's used to solitude. Before Tamio, he was alone all the time. Not that he's alone now. After all, he has me.

Mike visits Amber again during the week. There's a different nurse at the desk outside the Sun Room. She looks up at Mike as she tells him Amber's at a group activity.

Nurse: "Do you want me to fetch her?"

Mike: "No, that's okay."

Nurse: "You sure? She doesn't get many visitors." Mike wonders if the nurse actually sounds concerned.

Don't count on it.

Mike runs. He works out in his room. He is full of life. Everything is fantastic. Except for that time—

The knocking is intense.

Mom: "Mike! Mike! Open this door immediately!" She's pounding so hard, she could break the door down.

Mike is on the floor. He gets up, staggers over to the door, and unlocks it.

Mom: "Why'd you lock the door?"

Hasn't she ever heard of privacy?

Mom: "Why'd it take you so long to answer?"

Mike: "I didn't hear you."

Mom: "How could you not hear me? I was standing out there for God knows how long!"

Don't believe it. She only just started.

Mike finds himself back on the floor.

Mom: "Oh, my God." She's freaking out.

Mike: "Give me a second." He needs a moment to get his bearings.

Mom: "What if this happened while you were crossing the street?"

Mike: "Nothing happened."

You were tired. No big deal. You took a nap.

Mike: "It's no big deal. I took a nap."

Mom: "Where—on the floor?"

Mike: "Stop asking me stuff."

Mike tries to remember as his mom finally leaves him alone. He was going to do some push-ups. He can do 120 now. The floor rose up, Mike thinks; it was the weirdest thing.

It's not so weird. You were sleepy.

I can't really remember what happened, Mike thinks.

Because you fell asleep.

He can do 250 crunches now, too.

You are strong and getting stronger.

Mike knows he is. He can feel it. He looks in the mirror. He's so close to looking the way he wants to look, feeling the way he wants to feel. Having everything all under control.

I can be fit, Mike thinks. I can be strong. Infinitely strong.

You're almost there.

You and me both.

PART 3

STOP-MOTION

CHAPTER 23

MIKE WAKES UP AND HE KNOWS—HE JUST KNOWS—someone's been in his room. A trickle of panic runs down the back of his neck. He looks under his bed and in his closet; he checks the window, which is still closed as it is every night—it's too cold to leave it open. He can't find any evidence of theft, so he heads downstairs to the kitchen for a glass of water. But his mom is blocking the way.

Mom: "I have something to tell you."

Mike: "Later."

Mom: "Now. What I have to say, it's not open for discussion. It's happening whether you like it or not. I'm pretty sure you're not going to like it."

Mike: "What are you talking about?"

His mom is shaking. Why is she shaking? Mike wonders if it's because he used her credit card to buy Amber a bracelet. No, wait, he hasn't done that yet. Sometimes it's hard for Mike to tell the difference between actually doing something and just thinking about doing it.

Mom: "You're going to the hospital."

Mike: "Yeah, I visit Amber."

Mom: "You don't get it. You're the one going to the hospital. I'm having you admitted."

Mike: [nothing]

Mom: "Do you understand?"

Stay calm. Take a deep breath.

Mike (breathing deeply): "I don't need a hospital. I'm not sick."

Mom: "You blacked out."

Mike: "I took a nap!"

Mom: "Believe me, I've given this a lot of thought. In fact, it's all I've been thinking about."

So this is what she's been up to behind your back.

Mom: "It wasn't an easy decision, but it's the right one. I found a facility out of Belle Heights. It's not even in the city."

She wants to throw you out, like you're a piece of junk.

Mom: "I've done the research. It's a very good place. I haven't been, of course. You're not allowed to go, beforehand. You can only go as a patient."

That sounds suspicious.

Mom: "I packed you a bag."

Mike sees it near the couch, a small duffel like the one his dad took.

Mike: "Unpack it."

Mom: "I called an ambulance. It's on its way."

An ambulance; is she serious?

Mom: "The hospital suggested it. You might be too weak to walk."

Mike: "I run miles every day! How can I be too weak to walk?"

Mom: "I've been in close touch with your father."

She's not even listening to you.

Mom: "He was so upset when he saw you. He couldn't believe it—"

Mike: "Who cares?"

Mom: "Your physics teacher, Mr. Clayton, called me."

Mike: "I'm getting an A in physics, like in all my classes. What's the problem?"

Mom: "Mr. Clayton said there's no doubt in his mind you have an eating disorder."

Mike: "Is he a doctor, like Dr. Steiner, who said I was in excellent shape?"

Mom: "Tamio called me, too. More than once."

Mike: [nothing]

Tamio, the betrayer.

Mom: "Your baseball coach sent me emails. He heard from one of the kids that you quit the team."

Mike can't believe this. Are they all part of it?

They are all traitors.

Mike: "Well, guess what? I'm not going."

Mom: "It's not up to you. You're not eighteen. I'm the one admitting you, and you'll stay admitted until the staff says you're better."

She's not shaking anymore. She sounds strong. But she's never been strong. Mike's the one getting stronger, not her.

Mike: "How can you just pull me out of school in the middle of the year?"

Mom: "I spoke to your teachers. You can catch up on schoolwork over the winter break, if you're out by then."

How will I run, Mike thinks, how will I work out, what will happen to my body, my mind . . . ?

Think of Amber. She's getting through it. You will, too.

There's a knock at the door, and Mike's mom lets in two men in jumpsuits.

Ambulance man (to Mike): "Sit down. I have to take your heart rate and blood pressure."

Mike rolls up his sleeves. He has on two long-sleeved shirts and a sweatshirt. His mom bites her lip when she sees his arms.

Ambulance man (to the other one): "Get the wheelchair."

Mike: "Seriously?"

Ambulance man: "We didn't pull the ambulance up to your house in case you wanted to keep this private. We parked on the next street."

Mike: "I think I can walk one block."

Ambulance man: "You might not make it."

Mike: [nothing]

Ambulance man: "You've got bradycardia—your heart rate's forty-two. It should be seventy-five. You've got postural hypotension. That's low blood pressure. Your body temperature is ninety-two."

That can't be right. It's 98.6, like everybody else's.

Mike thinks the man is looking at him kindly.

Don't be fooled.

Ambulance man: "Those readings would be fine if you were hibernating."

Your mom was hibernating, not you. This is all wrong.

Then—unbelievably—the man lifts Mike up into his arms and carries him like a baby. Once they're outside, he places Mike in the wheelchair and pushes him on the bumpy concrete. Mike glances up and sees the bottoms of tree branches. He climbs into the ambulance and lies down. He looks at the ceiling. His mom is with him, clutching the bag she packed. They pull out into traffic. No siren. They just drive.

CHAPTER 24

MIKE HAS NO MEMORY OF SLEEP, BUT HE WAKES UP. Though it still feels more like dreaming than reality. Outside the ambulance, there are rolling green lawns like an endless golf course. There are no connected houses or apartment buildings. The sky is big, a cloudless, piercing blue that hurts his eyes.

Mom: "Did you sleep?"

You have nothing to say to her.

Mike: [nothing]

They stop and Mike gets out of the ambulance. They're in a circular driveway covered with dead leaves in front of a small building that looks more like a quaint country inn than a hospital. Mike could be here for brunch and tennis. A woman in a plaid dress with a bow at the waist greets Mike at the door.

Woman: "This is the central medical center. Here's where you get clearance."

Mike's heart starts racing. His forty-two-beats-a-minute heart.

He's taken into Admissions. He notices a grandfather clock with roman numerals. It has a steady tick. The furniture is upholstered with thick padding and the carpet has a diamond pattern. The lighting is soft. "Relax" seems to be the message. Mike is not relaxed. He's practically in shock. Someone tells him that he'll be the only boy in an eleven-bed wing, but that six months ago they had three boys at once.

They need a blood sample. An incompetent nurse tries to find a good vein, and she finally uses one on the back of Mike's hand.

Bad nurse: "You have shy veins, young man."

Shy veins and a lazy lip—Mike's body parts have so much personality.

Mom (with a quick hug, leaving): "See you later."

Mike: [nothing]

Another nurse takes Mike to a single room with yellow walls. There's a nurse at a desk just outside. Mike's window looks out on tall, leafless trees against the sky, a dark gray-blue now. It's quiet—no traffic, no airplanes. He can hear footsteps in the hall and footsteps overhead, a dull thumping. A nurse watches as he unpacks his bag—clothes, pajamas, toothbrush, toothpaste, deodorant. He feels like his possessions have betrayed him, following him here. The nurse unlocks his bathroom. There's a small mirror in there. Actually it's not really a mirror; it's some kind of reflective material, nonbreakable. It's as though he sees himself in a shimmery pool of water.

Another nurse shows up with a doctor's scale. She weighs Mike backward so only she can see the number. She slides up the bar that measures height.

Nurse: "You're five nine."

Mike: "And a half."

Nurse: "Not anymore."

How can I shrink? Mike wonders. I'm fifteen. Grandma Celia shrank when she was eighty.

It doesn't matter. Remember what's important. Inner growth.

A different nurse shows up and says she's taking Mike to the cafeteria. She locks Mike's door behind her. The cafeteria is nothing like the cafeteria at school or like the cafeteria at anybody's school. There are small round wooden tables, wooden chairs with cushions, and colorful rugs on a hardwood floor. Overhead, a glass chandelier clinks.

Mike: "I'm not hungry."

Nurse: "You have to eat six times a day."

Mike is stunned.

Mike: "What if I don't eat?"

Nurse: "You'll be hooked up to an IV. You'll be here a long, long time—a lot longer than four weeks."

That is unacceptable.

Mike's pulse races. He can't eat. He just can't. He thinks, What do I do?

You'll do what you have to do, to get out of here.

Nurse: "You start out on the liquid diet. You'll sit with other patients who are also on the liquid diet."

She leads Mike to a small table where three girls are drinking from large bottles labeled Ensure. Mike has heard of it. It's supposed to make you gain weight. Mike sits. He is given his own bottle. He can't bring himself to drink it. The nurse is watching him. Mike takes a sip. It tastes like strawberry milk. But—the whole bottle? It's not normal, he thinks.

It's the opposite of normal. But you have to. This is no time to be stubborn.

The girls introduce themselves—or at least two of them do. One is Cheryl and the other is Allison. Mike forgets which name belongs to which girl. One has olive skin and green eyes like his mom. The other is blond and has a long neck. They're not that thin, and Mike wonders how they ended up in an eating-disorder clinic. The third girl is the only one who looks thin. She's not drinking her Ensure. She has dark stringy hair that hangs in front of her face, and she stares ahead as if looking at something nobody else can see. It's like she's not here, Mike thinks.

She is somewhere else. That's brilliant. She's found a way to be herself, even in this hostile environment.

Cheryl or Allison (to Mike): "That's Nina. She doesn't talk much."

Nina. She reminds me of Amber. She's beautiful. Maybe a friend for Mike.

Nina is not like the others. Neither are you.

Cheryl or Allison: "Are you from around here?"

Mike: "Belle Heights." Blank stares. "It's in Queens, New York City."

Cheryl or Allison: "Oh, I love the city!"

Mike doesn't bother to tell them that Belle Heights isn't the city, not really. Cheryl and Allison talk about how much they love it, and one of them says she took a double-decker tour bus and actually looked in a second-story window and saw a guy in his underwear. Hilarious!

During the afternoon, Mike is taken to the rec room. Some kids are drawing; some are sculpting clay. One girl writes in a journal. Mike sits on an itchy couch.

That night, Mike lies on his bed and stares up at the ceiling. He thinks about doing crunches and push-ups, but his door has to stay open and there's a nurse right outside his room. He feels like he'll die if he can't work out.

Think of Nina. She's found a beautiful space for herself, away from here. You can do the same. You're running. The air fills your lungs. You are strong and getting stronger, infinitely strong. Now, dry your eyes.

Mike touches his face, surprised that it's wet.

CHAPTER 25

IN THE MORNING, MIKE STARTS THE ROUTINE.

• 7:00 a.m. Knock on the door (which stayed open all night).

Mike looks out the window and sees that all the dead leaves are gone. He must have slept deeply, right through the leaf blower.

I can't believe I'm here, Mike thinks. I don't belong here.

You are not really here. This is not your real life.

Strong body, strong mind, Mike thinks. Everything in its right place.

A nurse unlocks his bathroom and just stands there. He splashes cold water on his face. He doesn't look at his reflection. When he leaves the room, the nurse locks the door.

• 7:30–8:00 a.m. Breakfast.

A bottle of Ensure. Mike knows which name belongs to which girl now. Cheryl has green eyes and Allison's the blonde. Nina, silent, is far away.

• 8:15–8:45 a.m. Exercise class.

It's a joke. You sit on a hard floor and reach for your toes, then you stand up and bend. Mike looks around and sees that several girls have serious muscles and probably exercised for hours at home. But other girls seem to find even this amount of activity strenuous. One girl breathes so hard, Mike is afraid she'll pass out.

• 9:15–9:40 a.m. Personal time.

Mike sits on the enclosed porch, which overlooks the grounds. A nurse is at a desk just outside.

• 9:40–10:10 a.m. Snack.

Another bottle of Ensure.

Cheryl and Allison talk about missing their pets. Cheryl has a ten-year-old yellow Labrador who needs hip surgery, and Allison is deathly allergic to dogs but has a poodle because (it turns out) poodles have hair, not fur. Mike, bored, mentions his cat. Nina is smart. She doesn't say a word.

• 10:15–11:45 a.m. Group therapy.

Mike sits in a circle with ten girls from his wing and a doctor named Richard. Richard has a ponytail. He introduces Mike to the group. Then the girls talk. And talk. And talk.

One girl just got caught hiding high-fiber bars in her hair dryer where the batteries are supposed to be.

Girl who hid high-fiber bars: "Looking in my personal belongings constitutes illegal search and seizure."

Richard tells her that because high-fiber bars are laxatives, she has lost the privilege of walking the grounds tomorrow.

Another girl says she used to eat everything in sight and then throw up so much at home that all the pipes in her bathroom had to be replaced.

Girl who destroyed the pipes: "It cost a hell of a lot of money." She grins.

It makes no sense. Mike has such sublime control, and he's stuck here with girls who are nothing like him, compulsive girls who have zero control.

• 12:15–1:00 p.m. Lunch.

More Ensure.

Mike is starting to panic. He can't handle all this stuff in his system. He feels it, taking up space.

Amber was always such a big help. Maybe Nina can help you, too.

After Cheryl and Allison get up, Mike turns to Nina.

Mike (quietly): "Do you know a place I can go, to work out a little? Is there a room somewhere that's not locked, where they can't see you?"

Nina: [nothing]

Mike: "C'mon, tell me. Don't keep it a secret."

Nina: [nothing]

She would tell you, if she knew. She's on your side.

Nina looks down. Mike realizes he's got his hand wrapped around her forearm. He feels like he's holding a bone. He lets go.

• 1:15–2:30 p.m. Individual therapy.

It's Mike's first appointment with his one-on-one therapist. She looks Indian. She's not unattractive, with long dark wavy hair, a silky scarf around her throat, big eyes like a cat's, and jasmine perfume that fills the air. She sits on a couch, and Mike sits opposite her in an armchair.

Therapist (with a slight accent): "Hello, Mike. My name is Darpana." And she spells it for him: "D-a-r-p-a-n-a."

Mike: [nothing]

Darpana: "Do you know how sick you were, to be brought here?"

Remember Dr. Steiner? Tell her what she wants to hear. You didn't know what you were doing, but you're here now and you want to get well.

Mike: "I didn't know what I was doing. But I'm here now, and I want to get well."

Darpana looks at him. She might not be as stupid as Dr. Steiner.

Darpana: "Why do you think you went from one hundred fifty-four pounds last spring to one hundred three in November?"

Well, you needed to burn off a lot of fat. But you can't tell her that.

Mike: "Wow, that's really bad."

Darpana: "You were starving yourself, Mike."

Mike: "I was wrong to do that."

Darpana: "I saw the results of your blood test."

Don't listen anymore. She is not worth your attention.

Mike is able to tune her out. I listen, so he doesn't have to. Darpana says Mike's electrolyte levels are abnormal; his serum potassium levels are too low; the hair on his shoulders and stomach is called lanugo, and it sprouted, apparently, because Mike has zero body fat, and getting heat to the heart, lungs, and kidneys takes priority over the rest of the body, and the body is doing whatever it can to keep warm. She has no idea, of course, how good Mike felt, how the cold doesn't matter, how none of it matters when you're fit and strong, a master of chaos, in total control.

Darpana: "Are you listening to me, Mike?"

Mike: "Definitely."

• 3:00–3:30 p.m. Snack time.

More Ensure.

• 3:45 p.m. Walk around the grounds.

Everything feels unfamiliar, alien—how the air smells of trees, how the late-afternoon sun slants on rolling hills, leaving long shadows because winter is approaching. Back in Belle Heights, the only birds are pigeons and sparrows. Here the cardinals, blue jays, and crows are louder than any car alarm. Mike never thought he would miss the whoosh of planes and cars, or pigeons.

You are not really here. This is not your real life.

• 4:30–5:30 p.m. Activity period in the rec room.

Mike sees a girl at the drawing table, carefully choosing the color of a marker like she's deciding her future. Mike sits on the itchy couch. He wants to work out so badly. His body aches for it.

I was so close, Mike thinks. I was almost there.

• 6:00–7:00 p.m. Dinner.

More Ensure. Cheryl and Allison talk about food. Cheryl says she used to eat Sara Lee frozen cheesecake, still frozen, one sliver at a time. Mike notices something about Nina. Sometimes she whispers to herself.

• 7:30–9:30 p.m. TV in the rec room.

They watch reruns, flipping among *How I Met Your Mother* and

Mad Men and *Buffy the Vampire Slayer*.

- 9:45 p.m. Snack.

Mike drinks another bottle of Ensure.

- 10:30–11:00 p.m. Back to his room for another supervised visit to the bathroom, and quiet time.

Mike looks out the window. It's dark but the moon is bright. The hills look ghostly. This is not my real life, he thinks. I am not really here.

- 11:00 p.m. Lights out.

At some point later there's a powerful storm and it wakes Mike up. The rain beats against the window like it's trying to break through and spray Mike with cold water and shattered glass. He curls up beneath the blankets.

That therapist, Darpana, said I almost died, Mike thinks. She's seen patients die with better stats than me.

She was lying. She was trying to scare you. You're not like those patients. You are full of life.

Clearly the occasional stray remark is getting through to Mike. I'll have to be more diligent. No room for error here.

CHAPTER 26

WEEK TWO.

Mike goes through the routine. He is weighed backward. He drinks Ensure. Last Thursday—was it Thanksgiving? He barely noticed. No turkey for him, just more Ensure. He doesn't get visitors because this place discourages it. That's fine with Mike. The only people who would visit are the traitors who put him here.

He's moved to another table with Allison and Cheryl, while Nina stays at the old table. They have to eat what are called partials. The Ensure was bad enough, but this is real food and more than five bites of it. It's very tough for him. He puts a piece of toast in his mouth. It's like they're asking him to put his hand in a flame.

This is not my real life, Mike thinks while eating the toast. I am not really here.

You are running. Feel the cool air at the back of your throat. Nothing bothers you. Strong body, strong mind, infinitely strong.

Everything in its right place, Mike thinks.

Mike attends lectures on nutrition: "What the Body Needs, What the Body Wants."

Mike knows he doesn't have to pay attention. Amber knows way more than they do.

Darpana insults Mike's intelligence with her lies. She says that of the ten million people in this country who have eating disorders, 10 percent are boys and men.

That's one million guys, Mike thinks. Who is she kidding?

Just tell her that's an interesting statistic.

Mike: "That's an interesting statistic."

Darpana: "Huh. Not the way I would describe it."

Mike: "Right. It's scary. Very scary."

Darpana tells Mike why he has insomnia.

Darpana: "A Cro-Magnon man didn't sleep much—he was always thinking about getting the next meal. His senses had to be at full alert, so he could smell food that was ripe, see a small animal trying to hide in the bushes."

Can you imagine rummaging through the Dumpsters in Belle Heights, scavenging for food like a caveman? Don't listen to this nonsense.

Mike stops listening. Darpana goes into a whole thing about food rituals, and cuts and bruises that don't heal, and why eyes are sunken and lips are blue. Mike hears only the rhythm and cadence of her voice, the music of it; he nods or shakes his head based on the tone of her questions and statements; he says yes and no at all the right moments without knowing what he's saying yes or no to. He throws in the occasional "I understand" and "I can see that now."

Darpana: "I know about your speech problems as a kid. I know about your parents splitting up. I know you quit the baseball team. These things help me see you, Mike."

But she doesn't see Mike. And she never will.

Darpana says other things, too—obscene things. I won't repeat them now. I wish I didn't have to hear them in the first place and I certainly don't want to again.

One afternoon in group therapy, Richard asks everyone what they'd like to be when they grow up. It's the usual boring stuff.

Allison: "I want to invent a cure for allergies so I can be a vet."

Cheryl: "I'd like my own show on the Food Network."

Then, unexpectedly, something interesting happens. Nina speaks up for the first time.

Nina: "I want to be a plant." She has a soft voice, almost impossible to hear, a whisper of a voice. "I want to exist on nothing, taking nourishment from the air."

Richard: "We're talking about professions, Nina."

Of course Richard feels a need to criticize Nina instead of praising her for joining in the discussion. But Mike finds what Nina said a little creepy.

She's talking about death, he thinks.

No, she isn't.

Death is here, he thinks, like it's another person in the circle.

Does it never shut up, like the rest of them?

Mike thinks about Amber, how she said something about standing in the sun without casting a shadow, and moving so lightly she wouldn't disturb a spiderweb—

Amber is more alive than anyone you know.

Nina doesn't show up in the cafeteria that night. She stops coming to group therapy. Mike hears that she was caught throwing up and now she's in a private room, hooked up to an IV. This doesn't affect me one way or the other, but Mike takes it badly.

I have to work harder, then, to protect Mike from this place. Difficult and exhausting as it is, I do so willingly, of course. I don't mean to brag, but where would Mike be without me?

CHAPTER 27

WEEK THREE.

There's a new girl in group.

She's enormous.

Clearly she has no self-control, and Mike is appalled at her lack of discipline. A couple of girls roll their eyes at each other. One of them starts to laugh and has to cover her mouth. But it's not funny. This girl is their worst nightmare. Some have said they'd rather die than be fat. That's a little extreme, but I understand.

Richard: "This is Miranda."

Pretty name, Mike thinks, but it's the only pretty thing about her.

Miranda: "I know what y'all are thinking. I'm the fattest anorexic you've ever seen, right?"

First off—"y'all"? Is she Southern? What's she doing here? Secondly, her attempt at humor is completely lame.

Miranda: "Okay, I'm not really anorexic. I'm a compulsive overeater. And I make jokes when I'm incredibly nervous. Which I am right now. As if you can't tell."

If she thinks it's charming to make light about being disgusting, she's sadly mistaken.

But Mike feels a little bad for her. It's hard enough being here at all, but being a big girl like that—

She's revolting. You should have nothing to do with her.

Richard seems to find Miranda fascinating. He gets her to talk about where she's from (West Virginia) and about her family. I imagine they all look exactly like her, but to my surprise her mother was a beauty queen and her sister, Lydia, is one now.

Miranda: "When my mother was eight, she was Baby Miss America and there was a whole parade just for her. Lydia came in third for Miss Teen West Virginia. Which wasn't good enough, of course. When my sister loses, I know she and my mom blame me. Like the judges got a look at me and decided to punish Lydia."

She should just stay home, Mike thinks.

Locked in the cellar.

Cheryl: "So why do you go?"

Miranda: "My mom thinks it will inspire me to lose weight, seeing all those skinny girls parading around in bikinis." She grins. "I guess it hasn't worked, has it?"

Several girls can't understand why Miranda doesn't just throw up after eating.

Miranda: "Because I love feeling full. It's the only way I can sleep."

Girl who destroyed the pipes: "But throwing up is the best feeling in the world."

Miranda: "Maybe that's why my cat is always doing it. I don't know why I bother to put food in her dish. I should just put it directly on the floor."

A couple of girls smile at that. I don't find Miranda anything but hideous.

Mike doesn't talk much in group, but he says something every once in a while so he doesn't call attention to himself for his silence.

Mike: "My cat throws up a lot, too."

Miranda: "I thought I was the only one with a bulimic pet."

As they leave group, Miranda looks at Mike and says, "You and I have something in common."

Mike: "Because of our cats?"

Miranda: "We're like the answer to the question 'What's wrong with this picture?' I'm the fat girl among the skinny girls. And you're a boy."

To my horror Mike almost gets into a conversation with her, about feeling like the odd one out. He's lonely here—but of course he is! He doesn't belong here. This isn't his real life. He isn't really here.

This girl is a waste of your time.

Mike: [nothing]

Miranda: "See ya, I guess."

Mike takes off.

Later in the week, the girl who used to sit at the drawing table during activity period goes home, and Mike sits there now. He doesn't really draw, just sketches a little. I don't like it, but it's a small piece of time out of a long day.

Oh, no—the fat girl is here. She pulls up a chair and joins him.

Miranda: "Whatcha doin'?"

You have nothing to say to her.

Mike: [nothing]

Miranda: "It looks like bones."

Mike looks down at his paper. He thinks it does look like bones, now that she said so, but to me it's a bunch of meaningless shapes.

Miranda: "Is it some kind of animal?"

Mike: [nothing]

Miranda: "I like portraits. I like going to a museum and looking at the faces on the walls and wondering what the people in those paintings are thinking about. They had to sit there for hours, maybe days or weeks, you know? All they did was think. And the artist captured those thoughts, if you look carefully enough to see."

She's an idiot.

Mike is thinking about landscapes, about Ray Harryhausen's favorite artist, a French illustrator named Gustave Doré, who created dark, moody foregrounds and light-filled backgrounds. There's one image of a fallen tree with steps leading somewhere. Mike has always wanted to set foot on those steps, see where they go.

Miranda (pointing to his drawing): "Look at that. Your animal's got two heads. Cool."

Mike looks. Now he recognizes it. It's the two-headed Cyclops he drew all those years ago, when he first met Tamio.

Miranda: "Are two heads better than one?"

This is so boring.

Mike stands. He crumples up the drawing and tosses it away. He walks over to the itchy couch and sits there.

Good for you.

But Mike's thinking that maybe it was kind of rude to get up and leave—

Of course not.

—and he's sorry he threw away the drawing.

Don't be. It belongs in the garbage.

CHAPTER
28

Mike sits at a new table now, with Allison (Cheryl is still at partials) and a girl named Sandy who is instantly forgettable. He eats veggie burgers and tuna fish with mayonnaise. They're stuffing him like a piñata. He hates it, but he knows he'll take better care of himself at home and get his body back. For three weeks Mike has been putting up with a lot, and now the end is in sight.

Darpana: "You've got some wonderful qualities, Mike. Qualities to be proud of. You're smart and creative. A hard worker, a straight-A student."

Why is she complimenting you? She's up to something.

Mike: "Thank you. That's kind of you to say."

Darpana: "Everything that's good about you—anorexia loves it. Anorexia takes your intelligence and creativity and uses it to lie, repeatedly and convincingly, about why you don't eat, why you wear long underwear in the middle of summer. Anorexia uses that work ethic to force you to exercise even when you're famished and exhausted."

You can run over hunger, remember? And you felt great doing it.

I was so close, Mike thinks. I was almost there.

Darpana: "Anorexia takes a terrific person and turns him into a lying, moody, deceitful, self-centered manipulator."

In other words, an asshole.

Thanks a lot! Mike thinks.

Mike: "Yes, I wasn't myself."

Darpana takes out a blank piece of paper and a pencil. She draws a circle.

Darpana: "Mike, this is you, before the eating disorder."

Mike looks at the circle. To my discomfort, he is getting drawn in, so to speak. Darpana draws another circle next to the first one, and shades it in.

Darpana: "This other circle is the eating disorder. Now, as time goes by . . ." She draws another plain circle, partly covered by a shaded circle. "The circles begin to overlap. Until finally . . ." She draws another circle, this one almost completely covered by shading. The leftover plain part looks like a sliver moon. "Do you see? There you were." She points to the first plain circle. "Then came the eating disorder—the shadow." She points to the shaded circle. "The shadow covered you more and more, blocking out your light. You can barely see the first circle anymore. It's been eclipsed."

Mike: "I'm a shadow?"

Darpana: "Yes."

Mike: "I've been eclipsed?"

Darpana: "Yes."

Mike: "So—what you're saying—I'm not real."

Darpana: "The only real thing about you now is your eating disorder."

I can't believe Mike is upset about this. But this has happened before, more than once. I calm him down. He remembers this is not his real life and that he is not really here. He will go home and run, and nothing will bother him, and he'll get fit and strong, and he'll master the chaos.

They show an old movie in the rec room—*The Picture of Dorian Gray*. Generally I'm not a fan of movies because I don't see the point of sitting and staring when you could actually be doing something, but this one isn't too bad. It's about a good-looking man (Dorian Gray) who has his portrait painted, and the portrait has supernatural powers, so whenever Dorian commits an evil act, his portrait becomes more and more evil-looking. Dorian doesn't age but his portrait does. By the end of the movie, Dorian is still young and handsome but his portrait is old and hideous. It's some kind of cautionary tale, but I can't be bothered to figure out the moral.

In group the next morning, Miranda can't stop talking about the movie.

Miranda: "It got me thinking. I'm my mom's portrait."

Richard: "How so?"

Miranda: "My mom's terrified of gaining weight. So it happens to me—that way, magically, it doesn't happen to her. Ha, which gives me a great idea for a remake, y'all. A guy can eat and eat and stay thin, and his portrait gets fat for him. It could be called *The Eating Disorder of Dorian Gray*."

Some other girl: "I wish I had a portrait that could reach my IBW for me."

IBW—Ideal Body Weight. A little eating-disorder-clinic humor. It shocks me, how much the other girls like Miranda now. They tell her how beautiful her hair is, and how much they like her eyes, which are brown with yellow in them. She's repellant is what she is.

And Mike can't get rid of her at the drawing table.

He's been working on his two-headed Cyclops again, drawing in a ridged back and hairy legs, and carefully placing white dots in the eyes to indicate reflected light, something Tamio showed him how to do. But I'm sure he'll throw the picture away before going home.

Miranda: "He's awesome."

Mike: "Um . . . thanks."

Miranda: "Can he think two thoughts at the same time?"

Mike: "Huh?"

Miranda: "Well, he's got two heads. So maybe one head can look up and admire the moon, and the other head can think about his lonely childhood."

Mike: "His—what?"

Miranda: "I mean, look at him. He's a two-headed Cyclops among all the one-headed Cyclopses. He's a mutant in a race of mutants."

That's just about the dumbest thing I ever heard, but Mike is actually thinking about it.

Mike: "I guess if he has two heads, he'd have two voices . . . if he could talk, that is. Cyclopses usually just roar."

Miranda: "Two heads, two voices, two personalities; why not? They could be super close; they could hate each other. Whatever you want—he's your creature."

Mike: "You said 'creature.' You didn't say 'monster.'"

Miranda: "So?"

Mike: "That's what Ray Harryhausen always called them. He said the word 'monster' always made him think of Dracula."

Miranda: "Who's Ray Harryhausen?"

Amber never wanted to hear about Ray Harryhausen, and rightly so.

Mike: "Never mind."

Miranda: "No, go ahead. I'm interested."

I most certainly am not, and can barely listen as Mike talks . . . and talks . . . about how Harryhausen learned the craft of stop-motion animation from Willis O'Brien, the creator of King Kong. From the way Mike describes O'Brien, you'd think he cured cancer. Mike talks about how stop-motion can take a lifeless object and give it what Harryhausen called the "breath of life." How time-consuming it is: 24 adjustments to an object for just one second of film, which means 1,440 adjustments for one minute of film and 86,400 adjustments for one hour (yes, he has these numbers in his head). The adjustments are so small, Mike tells her, the eye can't see each one, but together they create movement.

Mike: "Harryhausen invented all kinds of strange, dreamlike creatures—giant bees, flying harpies, fire-breathing dragons.

He called them 'creatures from the mind.' But he always secretly hoped they were real. Except I know for a fact: creatures from the mind are real."

This is such a waste of time.

Mike: "Harryhausen always tried to give his creations a mind and a soul. He wants people to feel bad when they die."

Miranda: "I feel bad when King Kong dies."

Mike: "Me, too. Every time."

I'm almost dead with boredom by the time the conversation ends.

Finally, it's Mike's last night. He did what he had to do, and now he is allowed to go. He has reached 90 percent of his IBW. All that Ensure, all that food—Mike can't bear to think about it. He misses what he used to see when he looked in the mirror, the tightness of his skin, the clean lines of his body.

You're leaving, returning to your real life.

I was never really here, Mike thinks.

Mike sees Nina, for the first time in a long time. She's walking slowly down the hall, wheeling an IV pole attached to her arm. She has on the same kind of slippers that Mike used to see on Grandma Celia.

Mike walks over to her.

Nina: [whispers]

Mike: "What?" He leans in, close.

Nina smiles. Her teeth are gross, he thinks, and her breath is awful.

Nina: "Skin is soft, muscle is hard."

Mike: "Huh?"

Nina: "And bone is best."

Mike: "What are you saying?"

Nina: "Skin is soft, muscle is hard, bone is best."

Mike stares after her as she continues down the hall.

I don't want to end up like that, he thinks.

She is her own person, and you are your own person.

I don't ever want to come back here.

Not a problem. No one will know what you're doing. You'll be so careful.

I thought I was careful before—

You'll be even more careful.

Although going home presents some challenges. Mike is made aware that his mom will eat weekday breakfasts and dinners with him, and will take him to school and pick him up. Mike's dad will take over weekend lunches and dinners. In school he'll have lunch with Mr. Clayton in the physics lab. Mike is embarrassed by the fact that if he goes to the bathroom after lunch, Mr. Clayton has to go with him, to make sure he's not throwing up.

I don't do that, Mike thinks. I've never done that.

And once Mr. Clayton realizes it, he'll leave you alone. Soon enough they'll all get busy and you'll be on your own again.

After Christmas break, Mike has to go to therapy three times a week and family therapy once a week.

Where you'll tell them what they want to hear.

Mike thinks about how a special internist will weigh him once a week.

Remember the paperweights? The water loading?

Mike wonders if this special internist knows all the tricks.

There are always new tricks.

I'm not allowed to exercise. I can only take slow walks.

You can run when no one's looking.

If I break the rules, I come back. Darpana said it happens a lot. I could end up like Nina—

That's not going to happen. This place is history. That means the fat girl, too.

Miranda gave Mike her email and, after she gets home, wants him to write her.

You won't.

I promised, he thinks.

I don't remember him making any such promise. In any case, I tell him:

Promises in a place like this don't mean anything.

Mike packs his drawing of the Cyclops. I don't know why, and frankly at this point I don't care.

Mike's mom picks him up in a Lincoln Town Car from a car service. It's an improvement over the ambulance. Mike settles into the cushiony backseat.

Mom: "You look good."

Mike is surprised she can see. Her eyes are all wet.

As they drive away, Mike notices that the cut on his finger is all closed up. The scar is thin and faint, like a life line in the wrong place.

CHAPTER 29

IT'S GOOD TO BE HOME, BUT FRUSTRATING. MIKE HAS no privacy. It's like in the hospital except now it's his mom watching him. Even now she's right outside the door as he unpacks.

I can't work out, Mike thinks. How can I look in the mirror when there's a pair of eyes on me?

She has to sleep sometime, doesn't she? The middle of the night— the perfect time to get back on track.

In the meantime, she wants to watch a DVD with Mike—a Ray Harryhausen movie, something she's never done before. So they watch *Jason and the Argonauts*. Mighty Joe Young sits in Mike's lap and purrs like a jackhammer.

Mom (when the movie is over): "That's it? That's how it ends, with Jason kissing Medea?"

Mike: "Yeah."

Mom: "Do you know what happens to Jason and Medea?"

Mike (shaking his head): "They never made the sequel."

Mom: "Jason marries Medea and they have two sons. Then

he leaves her for the king's daughter. Medea is so filled with sorrow and rage and vengeance, she kills the new wife and even her own children."

Mike: [nothing]

Mom: "See, there are worse things than harpies and dragons. Jason and Medea—they're the real monsters."

What about parents who put their own children in the hospital when they're not sick?

When Mike goes to bed, his mom says he has to leave the door open.

Tell her you need some time alone. Do a few push-ups, at least.

Mike: "Can't you close the door for a little while?"

Mom: "No."

She stays with him until he falls asleep, and he sleeps so heavily, he doesn't wake up until the morning.

The next day Mike and his dad go to Luncheonette, the place with the rice pudding. They sit across from each other in a narrow booth. His dad orders a BLT for himself and a turkey club with fries for Mike. That's another hospital rule—Mike can't order his own meals. He feels like such a baby.

Why don't you just sit in a high chair?

Dad: "In case you're wondering, I'm still seeing Terry."

Mike: [nothing]

Dad: "You want to know how we met? At that old movie place—You Must Remember This. We'd just seen *The Picture of Dorian Gray*."

Mike: "I saw that movie too. At the hospital."

Mike's dad looks stricken. What, is Mike supposed to feel sorry for him now?

Mike: "Look, Dad, you don't have to say anything."

Dad: "No, I want to." Pause. "You always seemed fine, Mike. I mean, from the beginning. When you were born, I thought, Here's a fine, healthy kid. Even when you had problems with your speech, I never thought it was that big a deal. But I'm on board for you now, Mike. I hope you know that."

He's full of it. He's not on your side. He never was. He just said so himself.

Dad: "Anyway, after the movie Terry and I sort of walked out together and we started talking. We stopped in a coffee shop and split a spinach knish."

How romantic. Were there green bits in her teeth?

Mike smiles at that.

Dad: "Is something funny?"

Mike: "Private joke. Hey, you miss that girl you met at the gym?"

His dad hesitates.

Dad: "Honestly? When Laura walked into the gym, the whole place stopped. I miss how other guys looked at her and then over at me, enviously. That's the truth. I'm not proud of it."

Mike notices that his dad looks older, his eyes sadder and more deep-set. Mike can't help wondering if his dad used to think he knew himself, and now he's realizing how little he knew—

He's not worth thinking about. You have no use for him.

Dad: "Are you mad at me? I don't mean right this minute. I

mean, deep down. I wouldn't blame you if you were. Is that why you got sick, because I left?"

He's just like Amber's mom. It's all about him.

Mike: "That's not how it works."

Mike thinks his dad doesn't look reassured.

You're eating like a pig. Stop it.

Dad (pointing to the quarter sandwich Mike hasn't eaten): "You've got to finish that."

You should've put pieces of it in your lap. Well, just tell him you're full.

Mike: "I'm full."

Dad: "You have to eat it. I have to watch you eat every bite. I'm getting us a rice pudding, too."

Mike can't stand it—eating so much, not working out. He misses how good he used to feel, strong and getting stronger, infinitely strong.

This won't last. Your dad's not exactly the world's best parent, by his own admission.

CHAPTER 30

MIKE GOES BACK TO SCHOOL. HE'S NERVOUS, BUT I assure him that although he may be a novelty for a day or two, the effect will soon fade.

Ruby L: "Were you in the same place as Amber?"

Ruby C: "I heard she's not getting out until next year at the earliest."

Melissa Sacks: "I read about you in *Teen Vogue*. Well, not you specifically, but boys like you. You had manorexia, Mike."

Ralph: "I'll tell you what Mike had. He had it made! One guy and all those skinny chicks."

Mike: "Well, they're not all skinny."

Ralph: "You had it made. Damn!"

Mike notices that Ralph's newest T-shirt says TAKE ME DRUNK I'M HOME. He wonders why Melissa isn't on her cell phone reporting this to her PTA-president mom, but then Ralph puts his arm around Melissa and she snuggles into him. Mike can't believe it—they're going out.

Then he remembers that he doesn't care. They have nothing to do with him.

The coach catches up to Mike before homeroom.

Coach Jim: "Good to see you back. Too bad I can't use you this year, not if you can't make the winter workouts."

The coach is making it sound like a scheduling conflict, not like something Mike is absolutely forbidden to do. Anyway, Mike doesn't want to be on the team.

Coach Jim: "But I hope you'll come watch a few games. And I've got a senior playing center now, so I'll have a big hole there next year."

Didn't I always want to play center field? Mike thinks.

That was a long time ago, before you got your priorities straight.

Oh, no—Valerie.

She stands close to Mike. He inhales her flowery scent. He sees that tiny scar below her left cheek. His heart pounds in his chest.

Don't forget the kind of person she is.

She can turn on me, Mike thinks, at any moment.

Valerie: "Wow, your hair got long."

It's not so long; it brushes the back of his neck. He wasn't away for months on end, for heaven's sake.

Mike: "I guess I need a haircut."

Valerie: "No, it looks good."

First she compliments you, then she will turn on you. Just wait.

Valerie: "I'm really busy. I'm in a show in January—*Sleeping Beauty*. I'm not the lead or anything, but I've got rehearsals all the time. I love it, though. Someday I hope to choreograph—if not ballet then modern." She clears her throat. "Okay, that's not really what I wanted to say. I just—Mike, I see it a lot, at dance. Kids who get so thin, they're not strong enough to dance. But I never thought of it with you." She looks at him, hesitates, and squeezes his arm. It's a rather strange gesture. She holds on. It reminds Mike of that time she took his arm. It's like she never let go, he thinks.

This girl is so utterly not on your side.

The bell rings. She dashes off.

Mike sees Tamio. Tamio betrayed me, Mike thinks.

Move on.

Mike starts walking, but Tamio follows him.

Tamio: "Wait. Want to get lunch later?"

Mike: "I have to eat in the lab with Mr. Clayton."

Tamio (walking beside him): "I know, your mom told me. I hope it's okay I've been talking to her. You know, over the past month. To see how you were doing."

It's not okay. He has no right to spy on you like that.

Tamio: "I got my lunch period changed. It's all right with Mr. Clayton if it's all right with you."

Mike: [nothing]

Tamio takes off in the other direction. Of course he's interpreting Mike's silence as a yes. Because that's what Tamio wanted to hear. They're all alike—they only hear what they want to hear.

Lunch is weird, as I knew it would be.

Mr. Clayton is on his computer and Tamio and Mike sit there in silence. Mike eats a grilled-cheese sandwich and drinks a bottle of Ensure. He still has to drink three of those a day, plus three meals and two snacks. It's enough food for an army.

Tamio: "I saw something on YouTube you'd like."

Mike: "Yeah?"

Tamio: "These two guys made a stop-motion movie of how they built a *Millennium Falcon* out of Legos. The animation is seamless."

Something sparks inside Mike. I love this stuff, he thinks, don't I?

No, you used to love it. Things change.

Mike: "How long is the video?"

Tamio: "Just under three minutes."

Mike: "How long did it take them?"

Tamio: "Thirty-eight hours."

Mike: "That's not bad."

Tamio: "It got me thinking. We could make a stop-motion movie. My dad just got a special camera that can shoot single frames. I got some special software, too, that helps you line up the camera and go back and forth between images so you can make sure it all looks good."

You don't have time.

Mike: "I'm behind on all my homework, in case you didn't know."

Mr. Clayton glances up from his computer.

Mr. Clayton: "Mike, Tamio's got a great idea. As animators,

you'd have to take measurements, study movement and perspective. I think this movie would be perfect for you and Tamio as a year-end project."

Tamio: "Cool! We can invent our own creature and film it."

Oh, I understand now. They've been plotting this—just the way they plotted to send Mike to the hospital.

Don't do it. Don't do it. Don't do it.

But I have to do it, Mike thinks. Thanks to Mr. Clayton, now it's homework.

Finally Mike has an opportunity to visit Amber in the Sun Room. His dad has to take Mike to the hospital and will sit in the cafeteria until it's time to take Mike home again. It's like Mike is in a prison whose walls are everywhere. But at least he gets to see Amber.

She looks good, Mike thinks; her eyes are clear, her hair's shiny, there's color in her face.

Amber (biting off her words): "Thanks for coming to see me. Where the hell have you been?"

Mike: "You'll never guess. Okay if I sit down?"

Amber: "I really don't care."

The padded chair is as hard as Mike remembers. She's in a bad mood, he thinks.

Can you blame her? She missed you.

I missed her too, Mike thinks with some surprise. He realizes, maybe for the first time, how much he cares about her. Well, it took him long enough.

Amber: "Did you get my bracelet?"

Mike: "Sorry. No."

Amber: "Thanks a lot. It's the one thing I asked you to do."

Mike looks around the Sun Room. There are some hand-drawn pictures of sunrises and sunsets taped to the wall.

Mike: "I was in a hospital. Like this one."

Now he has her attention.

Amber: "You're kidding."

Mike: "Nope. I was really, truly there." As he says this, the weight of it hits him. I thought I was with people who were nothing like me, Mike thinks, people who had no control over themselves. But am I any different?

You're badly confused. No doubt because you're in a hospital setting. It's warping your judgment.

Amber: "Were the girls there skinnier than me? I bet you didn't even notice. Did you eat everything they put in front of you? There's no way I'd do that. I'd explode."

Mike: "You look good."

Amber: "I don't! I'm disgusting."

Mike: "How close are you to your IBW? Look at me, I speak the language."

Amber: "You mean my Insane Body Weight? That's what Deirdre calls it."

Mike: "How's she doing?"

Amber: "She's not my roommate anymore. She's down the hall, on a feeding tube. She needs potassium. So I've got my own room until they stick somebody else in there. My mom wants to keep me in a single. She thinks the other girls are a bad influence. She's such a bitch. Miss Cool Hunter! She'll never understand. What's cooler than being thin and happy and living life the way you want to live it?"

Mike: "You can't live it if you're dead."

I am . . . appalled. I can't believe Mike just said that. I don't think he can believe it, either. He sounds like Darpana, with her obscene talk of death and dying, which I listened to so Mike wouldn't have to.

Amber: "Excuse me?" She's not saying this because she didn't hear Mike, but because she also can't believe it.

Mike: "I'm on your side, Amber."

Amber: "You wouldn't know it!"

Mike: "I don't want you to, you know, die."

Of course you don't. But this isn't what Amber needs to hear right now.

Amber (glaring at him): "An extra pair of eyes on me—is that what you're gonna be, Mike? I don't want that. I don't need that." She looks out the window, but it's dark. There's nothing to see.

Apologize.

Mike: "I barely know you, Amber."

That is not what I had in mind.

Amber: "You know me! You've known me since kindergarten."

Mike: "Yeah, I remember when you were little. You were always—"

Amber looks horrified. She's not sure what Mike is about to tell her about herself.

Mike: "—really smart. You knew the answers before anyone else."

Amber takes a deep breath.

Mike: "I've got to go, but I could come back next Monday. Maybe you could tell me about your aunt and stuff."

Amber: "What is wrong with you?"

I'd like the answer to that question myself.

Amber: "Anyway, next Monday is Christmas."

Mike: "I know."

Amber: "Don't you have something else to do?"

Mike: "Nothing I'd rather do."

Amber half smiles. Mike has never seen that before. It's not one of her sneaky smiles.

CHAPTER 31

MIKE BRINGS HIS PICTURE OF THE TWO-HEADED Cyclops to lunch on Friday, right before Christmas break. He remembers, as a kid, watching the Cyclops (with only one head, naturally) in *The 7th Voyage of Sinbad*. That Cyclops couldn't talk but he could roar, and Mike loved and admired him for that; nobody misunderstood him or asked him to repeat himself.

You're not a little kid with a speech problem anymore. You're an entirely different person now.

Mike (showing Tamio the drawing): "What do you think?"

Tamio: "You drew something like this a long time ago, didn't you?"

Mike: "Would he be too hard to make? Maybe something with Legos would be easier."

Tamio: "We can use clay."

Mike: "If you want to design a different creature—"

Tamio: "He's great. He's perfect. Oh, I forgot to tell you. Val wants to work on the movie too."

This is not good.

Mike: "What?"

Tamio: "I told her you and I were doing a movie. She likes stop-motion."

Mike: "She knew what it was?"

Tamio: "She's a big fan of Wallace and Gromit."

Mike: "And you told her I was doing the movie too?"

Tamio: "Yeah. Like I said."

Mike: "But she doesn't have time. She's always at dance."

Tamio: "We have to start without her, but once her show ends, she'll join us. It'll be her physics project, too."

Mike: "You sure you said it was me?"

Tamio: "Yes! For the third time."

Mike is thinking about stop-motion, how slow and careful and precise it is; you have to get it exactly right so it looks smooth, not choppy; you need to work together closely; he and Valerie, working together, close—

She's unstable. She'll turn on you.

When I saw her, Mike thinks, she didn't turn on me.

Because she was too busy talking about herself. Could she be more self-centered?

Tamio: "You wanna come over later? We can pick up some clay and make the model. What do you think—film in black and white or color?"

Tamio starts talking about the advantages of black and white versus color, or vice versa; how in a black-and-white movie you can use ink for blood and it looks authentic, but color in general is better, and Tamio says he can get his hands on some really good fake blood called Kensington Gore, which, if you add glycerine to it, thickens like the real thing. Then Tamio starts talking about Japan, how he met some girl there; he didn't think much about it, but now she might visit the city with her parents over Christmas break. . . . Tamio's acting as though he just got back from Japan and the past four months never happened.

But they did so happen. I am living proof.

Mike goes to Tamio's after school, though Tamio has to call Mike's mom first and assure her that Mike will have a snack: oatmeal cookies and a milkshake. If Tamio had any character to speak of, he'd let Mike off the hook, but he's such a spy and traitor, he'll probably force-feed Mike himself.

Tamio's mom makes a big fuss over Mike. If it were me, I'd find it embarrassing and over-the-top, but Mike doesn't seem to mind it, even when she gives him a crushing hug (she's a lot stronger than she looks). She keeps saying how happy she is to see him; meanwhile she has a look of tragedy on her face.

Mike and Tamio work in the dining room, Mike's favorite place in Tamio's house—it's always sunny, or it feels that way to him, surrounded by pictures of flowers and actual flowers on the table too—carnations. I don't understand the appeal of flowers. They rot so quickly; what's the point? Beauty should have permanence.

Tamio's mom puts waxed paper on the table so they can spread out the clay they got at an art-supply store, a huge gray mound of it. The model for the original King Kong was eighteen inches tall, except for full-scale models of the head, a hand, and a foot; Mike and Tamio want to emulate that and make the Cyclops eighteen inches tall. Of course it won't have a metal skeleton the way Kong did, with foam rubber and latex and rabbit fur so it looked like a real gorilla. This thing will probably look, heaven help me, like Gumby.

Tamio: "Ralph and Melissa. Did you ever think that would happen?"

Mike: "Not in this lifetime."

They talk about Ralph and Melissa for a while, and I can barely stay with them. Then they concentrate on their movie. They decide that the heads will be like those of fraternal twins, not identical ones. Tamio will sculpt one head and Mike will do the other. Mike has never handled modeling clay before, having preferred to be a disc jockey rather than sit with the other kids at the art table. He likes the feel of it in his hands, the slightly outdoorsy smell of it, how it's soft, but firm enough to hold its shape, adjustment after adjustment.

Walking. That's the first thing they decide to film—the Cyclops walking. What does a body do when it takes a step; how do the muscles interact, the arms move, the shoulders, neck, hips? Apparently this is very complicated. Of course Mike should be running, not worrying about how a Cyclops walks.

Tamio (sculpting his head): "Does he have a name?"

Mike: [nothing]

Tamio: "Harryhausen always said his creatures should have some character."

Mike remembers what Miranda said about his Cyclops's loneliness: a mutant in a race of mutants.

Mike: "Let's call him Ray."

Tamio (grinning his crooked grin): "Harryhausen would be honored."

They talk about the story. Ray needs to fight someone or something. Should they create another creature, this one with thumbs and a big head, because, as Tamio points out, Harryhausen said creatures with thumbs and big heads appear more human, and therefore more intelligent?

I am growing numb with boredom. I would tear my hair out, if I had hair.

Tamio: "We can use your cat. Film Mighty Joe Young clawing at something, then cut to shots of Ray."

The cat? This is so ridiculous, I actually have to tune them out. I don't do that as a rule, but even I have my limits, and it's not like I have to stand guard every second. Mike has to do this for school, and I can get him when he's free again.

When I catch up to them, Mike is putting the finishing touches on his clay head, adding what looks like a ridged eyebrow over the one eye.

Mike: " . . . my idea. Ray has two heads. He has two voices. What if he has to fight one of his own voices?"

Wait—what? What is Mike saying?

Tamio: "What's wrong with the voice?"

Mike: "Maybe one of the heads is suddenly possessed—by an evil spirit or something. Ray's a creature, but this thing inside him is a monster, you know? It says stuff. It gets Ray to do things he shouldn't. It acts like it's Ray's best friend, but really it wants to kill him."

I am far more angry with myself than with Mike. This never would've happened if I'd stayed alert.

Mike: "You can only see the monster in a mirror. It looks like— a skeleton head."

Tamio: "Cool."

Mike: "The problem is, how do you get rid of it? How do you stop a voice?"

Tamio: "Give me a minute."

Do you realize how crazy you sound? Look at Tamio—he thinks you're crazy. He'll call your mom. She's probably already on his speed dial. Next thing you know, you're back in the hospital.

Tamio: "There's a pit, okay? A pit of voices. Ray has to lead the voice to the pit. When he gets closer, he can hear all the voices inside, overlapping and trying to be heard, but now they're stuck in the pit, and anyway there's too many to listen to and you can't make out any single voice anymore. Ray has to leave the voice in the pit."

Mike: "How?"

Tamio: "Being near the pit of voices will help. It's clear that once there, the voices are in a weakened, powerless state."

Mike: "And once the voice is in the pit?"

Tamio: "It's trapped."

Mike: "What if it breaks free?"

Tamio (nodding): "It might do that." Pause. "Then we'll come up with something else."

You and me both, Tamio seems to be implying. Well, he's sadly mistaken. This is only a movie, with a totally imaginary voice as a villain. Whereas I am good for Mike; I am on his side; I won't betray him, like everyone else. This pointless project means no more to Mike than doing a few algebra equations, soon forgotten.

CHAPTER

32

MIKE AND HIS DAD ARE IN SPRUCE HILLS ON Saturday, two days before Christmas, heading for the mall. The streets are so crowded with shoppers that they're constantly edging out of the way of people with giant overstuffed plastic bags and shiny packages. Snow is coming; the sky is blindingly white; it's chilly, but Mike has his jacket open. He likes feeling this way, not so cold.

The cold doesn't matter when you're getting fit and strong.

Then Mike sees her—a woman with spiky black hair.

Mike: "I know that woman."

Dad: "Who?"

She's standing right in front of them as if they had all arranged to meet at this exact spot at this exact moment. It's that client of Mike's mom. What was her name again? Meg.

Keep walking. You have nothing to say to this woman.

But she recognizes Mike too, or thinks she does. She smiles, and her expression is asking a question: Do I know you?

Mike: "I'm Mike Welles. You hired my mom to clean out your closet."

That smile of hers fades fast.

Mike: "This is my dad."

They shake hands.

Meg: "Your mother called me. She was nice. She wanted to reschedule, wasn't going to charge me. But . . . I don't know."

Mike: "What about me?"

Meg: "What about you?"

Mike: "I've worked with my mom. I know how to clean out closets."

Have you lost your mind?

Dad: "Seriously?"

Even your dad thinks you're crazy.

Meg (looking confused too): "You want to make an appointment to clean out my closet, is that it?"

Mike: "We're not far from where you live, right? How about now?"

I don't understand this at all. What is Mike up to? What does he imagine this will accomplish?

Meg: "What do you think, Mr. Welles?"

Dad (looking at Mike carefully): "I think he wants to do this."

Mike nods.

You can't possibly mean it.

Dad: "So I'll see you at home for dinner at six, okay? If you get hungry, here's an energy bar."

Mike's dad sounds like an ordinary dad. Mike is grateful that his dad isn't broadcasting the fact that his son must eat this snack because he was just released from a hospital.

Mike (like an ordinary kid): "Later."

But this is not ordinary, far from it. Prisoner Mike, he should be called. They walk to Meg's place. And . . . wait. I get it. Mike just broke out of prison! Maybe Mike didn't plan it this way or maybe he did—either way it's brilliant.

You just got rid of your dad. Now you can get rid of her, too.

Mike knows it. He hasn't been alone in weeks, always someone hovering over him, shoving a bottle of Ensure down his throat, keeping an eye on him, even when he's in the bathroom. Mike takes a deep breath. The air fills his lungs. He can run, catch up on his running, make up for all the time he couldn't run. I can be fit, Mike thinks. I can be strong, infinitely strong.

Yes! Go!

But, he thinks, my dad trusts me.

So what? You don't have to trust him. He hasn't earned your trust.

I don't want to lie to him.

Lying can be necessary. Lying can protect you.

No, Mike thinks, that is not the purpose of a lie.

To my dismay, Mike follows Meg through her lobby to the elevator. This stubbornness of Mike's—it's always been a problem.

Mike separates the stuff into three categories: keep, throw away, donate. A navy-blue blazer and an alarm clock, still in its unopened box, get to stay. Into the garbage go a battered suitcase with no handle, and some coats and dresses with zippers that don't zip. For the Salvation Army, there's an endless supply of skirts, sweaters, and jeans, and a tennis racket, a printer, and a popcorn maker.

As Mike reaches the back of the closet, he sees something. It startles him—it's a face, staring back. It takes Mike a moment to realize that he's looking at his own reflection in a small mirror with a silver frame.

Is that me? Mike thinks. It looks like me.

Of course it's you. Who else would it be?

Darpana—she said I wasn't real. I was eclipsed, a shadow, a trick of the light.

She never said that. Anyway, a trick of the light is an honest mistake. Could happen to anybody.

A trick of the light is a lie, Mike thinks. A lie you tell yourself. And you still try to get away with it.

Mike: "Look, there's a mirror here."

Meg (peering into the closet): "Oh, right. I forgot I had it."

Mike: "Is it valuable?"

Meg: "Not at all."

Mike: "Can I have it? I've got a mirror at home, but it's warped and I'm getting rid of it. I want to replace it."

This mirror is too small. How will you see yourself? Don't be idiotic.

Funny, how the voice can sound like Grandma Celia, Mike thinks, finding fault, criticizing—

Now that's just insulting.

This mirror's the perfect size for the movie, Mike thinks. Ray can see his reflection, the monster within—

Forget the movie! Remember how good you used to feel? You were so close. You were almost there.

Close—to what? Almost where?

You were so full of life.

It seemed like it.

Listen to yourself!

I'm trying to, Mike thinks.

It takes Mike another hour to clean out the closet. Meg tries to give him money, but he won't let her. He'll take only the mirror. They argue about this for a while, but Mike insists.

Meg: "Can I tell my friends about you? You could make some good money."

Mike: "Thanks, but I'm really busy these days. You could tell people about my mom. She'd appreciate the word of mouth."

Mike carefully wraps the mirror up with newspaper and tape, like it's a Christmas present. He heads outside. It's snowing lightly, so lightly it almost isn't snowing. Mike finds the almost-snow beautiful.

Run home. No one will know.

I can't run, he thinks, I'm holding the mirror.

You're full of excuses! Drop it in the garbage, where it belongs.

The voice in my head, Mike thinks: if I don't listen to it, can it speak?

Why shouldn't you listen? Everyone else has betrayed you. They will betray you again. You need to work on yourself. When you get home, look in the mirror—the one you can trust. You can get your body back. Strong body, strong mind, strong enough to master the chaos—

Mike (aloud): "Oh, just leave me alone already."

I'm shocked to my core. I'd be shaking if there were anything to shake. This is the first time Mike has spoken to me like that, in his own voice. And what a thing to say. He doesn't sound angry or afraid. He just sounds . . .

. . . distant.

But I will not leave him alone. That is not what's best for him.

Mike is thinking about what Harryhausen said: how, when his creations die, there's sadness because each one has a mind and a soul.

Mike gets on the Q22 bus home. It's crowded, but he spots a seat near the back. He sits holding the mirror. Beside him, there's a man on a cell phone. Behind him, a woman gets a call. Then several other people make calls.

Man next to Mike: "Speak up. I can't hear you."

Woman behind Mike: "There's somebody talking really loud right in front of me—what'd you say?"

Mike (to me in his head): "Guess what? You're in the pit of voices."

[nothing]

It takes me a moment, but of course there's no such thing as a pit of voices. It's just the boring Belle Heights bus with a bunch of obnoxious people talking loudly on cell phones. I let Mike know

I'm still here, that this bit of treachery didn't just wipe me out of existence. I tell him:

You can be strong, infinitely strong.

So it won't be easy, Mike thinks, but it's a step in the right direction—even if it's smaller than the eye can see.

AUTHOR'S NOTE

SOME YEARS AGO, I READ AN ARTICLE CALLED "NOT for Girls Only" in the New York *Daily News*. It was about a boy with an eating disorder. I never knew boys could develop eating disorders, and this idea was so unexpected, it took hold of me and wouldn't let go. How does a boy become anorexic? Is it different from what happens with girls?

I emailed the reporter and then spoke with the boy in the article, his family, and his doctor, who put me in touch with other families. I met several young men and their parents. I did research on the complex world of eating disorders, visiting hospitals and reading many excellent books, both fiction and nonfiction (please see the list, below).

As Mike learns in this book, of the 10 million people in the United States with eating disorders, 10 percent are male (and some reports put this figure even higher). That's one million boys and men, an epidemic that is, as one writer puts it, "overlooked, understudied, and underreported" because "it's a girl's disease." Yet the first two documented cases of eating disorders, back in the 1600s, involved a girl and a boy. It wasn't called anorexia nervosa back then—that term, which originated in the 1800s, translates to "lack of desire to eat" or "nervous loss of appetite." Which isn't really accurate. There is tremendous desire to eat and no loss of appetite. But eating disorders have ways of manipulating the truth.

Anorexia, bulimia, and other eating disorders have the highest death rate of any psychological disorder—though I'm very pleased to say that all the young men I interviewed for this book are doing exceptionally well. One of the moms recently emailed me, triumphantly, her son's healthy weight.

—Lois Metzger

February 2013

Andersen, Arnold, Leigh Cohn, and Thomas Holbrook. *Making Weight: Healing Men's Conflicts with Food, Weight, Shape & Appearance*. Carlsbad, CA: Gürze Books, 2000.

Anderson, Laurie Halse. *Wintergirls*. New York: Viking, 2009.

Brown, Harriett. *Brave Girl Eating*. New York: William Morrow, 2010.

Bryant-Waugh, Rachel, and Bryan Lask. *Eating Disorders: A Parents' Guide*. Rev. ed. New York: Brunner-Routledge, 2004.

Costin, Carolyn. *The Eating Disorder Sourcebook*. 2nd ed. Los Angeles: Lowell House, 1999.

Gottlieb, Lori. *Stick Figure: A Diary of My Former Self*. New York: Berkley Books, 2001.

Harryhausen, Ray, and Tony Dalton. *An Animated Life*. Foreword by Ray Bradbury. New York: Billboard Books, 2004.

Hautzig, Deborah. *Second Star to the Right*. New York: Puffin Books, 1999.

Hendricks, Jennifer. *Slim to None: A Journey through the Wasteland of Anorexia Treatment*. New York: McGraw-Hill, 2004.

Hornbacher, Marya. *Wasted: A Memoir of Anorexia and Bulimia*. New York: HarperPerennial, 1998.

Kandel, Johanna S. *Life Beyond Your Eating Disorder*. Ontario, Canada: Harlequin, 2010.

Levenkron, Steven. *The Best Little Girl in the World*. New York: Warner Books, 1979.

Lock, James, and Daniel Le Grange. *Help Your Teenager Beat an Eating Disorder*. New York: The Guilford Press, 2005.

———, W. Stewart Agras, and Christopher Dare. *Treatment Manual for Anorexia Nervosa: A Family-Based Approach*. New York: The Guilford Press, 2001.

Medoff, Jillian. *Hunger Point: A Novel*. New York: Regan Books, HarperCollins, 2002.

Menzie, Morgan. *Diary of an Anorexic Girl: Based on a True Story*. Nashville: Thomas Nelson, 2003.

Sacker, Ira M., and Marc A. Zimmer. *Dying to Be Thin: Understanding and Defeating Anorexia Nervosa and Bulimia: A Practical, Lifesaving Guide*. New York: Warner Books, 2001.

Sparks, Beatrice, ed. *Kim: Empty Inside: The Diary of an Anonymous Teenager*. New York: HarperTeen, 2002.

Vizzini, Ned. *It's Kind of a Funny Story*. New York: Miramax Books, Hyperion Paperbacks, 2007.

Ten Things You Probably Didn't Know About Eating Disorders

1. The National Eating Disorder Association estimates that 30 million people in this country have eating disorders at some point in their lives.

2. Children as young as five have been diagnosed with eating disorders.

3. The mortality rate for eating disorders can be as high as 20 percent. Causes of death include electrolyte imbalance, heart failure, dehydration, hypoglycemia, kidney failure, and suicide.

4. The "Maudsley Approach" to eating disorders, also known as family-based treatment, has seen much success in recent years. According to *U.S. News & World Report*, it "emphasizes recovery over cause, and care provided by parents, not by doctors."

5. Bulimia, the eating disorder characterized by binge eating and purging (throwing up), literally means "ox-hunger."

6. Wrestlers are particularly susceptible to eating disorders because they have to "make weight," and mistakenly believe that competing in a lower weight class will give them an advantage. For rapid weight loss before a weigh-in, up to three-quarters of high school and collegiate wrestlers will overexercise, fast, and restrict fluids.

7. There is evidence of a genetic component to eating disorders, meaning that some people may have a biological vulnerability. Scientists have discovered two gene mutations that have been linked to a higher-than-normal risk of developing an eating disorder.

8. This book is fiction, but the narrator—also known as the "eating-disorder voice" or the "anorexic voice"—is very real. It's been described in other books (fiction and nonfiction) as, for example, an ever-present "green, scaly creature with a large beak," "the dictator," "the beast," "a drumbeat, a howl," and a voice that "didn't seem to be me doing the talking. Not any part of me I'd ever encountered, anyway."

9. Chances are you know someone with an eating disorder.

10. If you want to help, it's important to take action quickly because eating disorders can escalate fast and are so deadly. A good first step is calling the National Eating Disorder Association hotline: 1-800-931-2237.

ACKNOWLEDGMENTS

MANY THANKS TO:

My agent, Susan Cohen at Writers House, for her enthusiasm, kindness, and belief in this book, which is dedicated to her.

Her assistant, Brianne Johnson, who helped enormously with her insights and suggestions.

Kevin Webb, who was an intern at Writers House and who read an early draft and helped bring the book into focus and worked with me even after he left Writers House. He has an amazing eye and ear for story and language.

At Balzer + Bray, I am very grateful to Alessandra Balzer and Donna Bray, and to Renée Cafiero, Alison Donalty, Ray Shappell, and Viana Siniscalchi.

The following people also helped along the way:

Jacob Hiss; Tony Hiss; Katharine L. Loeb, PhD, at Fairleigh Dickinson University and Mount Sinai School of Medicine; Rachel Lisberg; Dr. James Lock, an expert on eating disorders at Stanford

University; Gail Monaco; Julie Patel, former San Jose *Mercury News* reporter and current *Sun-Sentinel* reporter; Justin Roberts; Susan Roberts; and Niobe Way, professor of applied psychology at New York University.

I thank my lucky stars for my editor at Balzer + Bray, Jordan Brown. He is a spectacularly nice person, and funny and smart and warm, as well as a tremendously gifted editor. He helped give this book a mind and a soul.